As the Sparrows Fly
B.L Blocher

Copyright © 2021 B.L Blocher

All rights reserved. No part of this book may be reproduced or transmitted in any form or by any means, electronic or mechanical, including photocopying, recording or by any information storage and retrieval system without permission in writing from the publisher.

The Emerald City Press—Southington, CT
ISBN: 978-1-7374610-1-2
Library of Congress Control Number: pending
Title: As the Sparrows Fly
Author: B.L Blocher
Digital distribution | 2021
Paperback | 2021

This is a work of fiction. The characters, names, incidents, places, and dialogue are products of the author's imagination, and are not to be construed as real.

Thewatchmaker1939@gmail.com

Dedication

I'd like to dedicate this story to our incredible goldendoodle Tasha. She helped raise our two children and was absolutely the kindest and sweetest dog. She was a special blessing to our family.

Sadly, we miss her greatly, but her wonderful spirit lives on through her daughter Trixie, who we love and cherish more than anything.

I would also like to give an honorable mention to "Stewie," our Morgan horse who carried both of my children to victory after victory.

And to Europa, who was the greatest horse I ever owned. He was once ranked #2 in the nation, but in our hearts he will always be #1.

May you all rest in peace my beloved friends and frolic in greener pastures.

Other novels by B.L Blocher

The Watchmaker

The Watchmaker 2

The Silver Orchid

Razzle Dazzle

Introduction

Almost everyone has had some dastardly experience while growing up with their siblings. Often it was just typical outright Darwinism, "survival of the fittest," and other times maybe just a little friendly competition of vying for mom & dads attention.

I'm not portraying in any way that all siblings or sibling rivalries were a nefarious thing, unless of course it turned vicious or even toxic.

However, on the other hand, many if not most siblings do cherish one another and form everlasting bonds of love and devotion towards each other, but that wouldn't be as much fun to read or write about. I believe that this story just might strike a chord and one might look back and rememorize the good, the bad and the ugly times of their childhood, and either dismally relate to it, or enjoy the fact that they were one of the lucky ones that grew up in a Brady Bunch family. The dynamics of sibling relationships were always complicated and seemed to be present ever since the beginning of time.

One of my favorite biblical stories from the Old Testament is the story of Joseph. Where a fathers blatant favoritism to a certain son in a cast of 12 brothers didn't fare very well with any of them, and they made a plot to get rid of their favored "Robe of Many Colors" brother, Joseph. In the end they patched things up, however the 12 brothers ultimately split up and spread their 12 tribes of Israel all around the world. The scholars who wrote that infamous biblical story recognised the fact that sibling relationships are not always going to be perfect, but there is always a possibility for reconciliation. That is unless your names are Cain and Abel....then not so much.

Growing up on a farm, I actually did have older siblings.

However, this is not an autobiography and is in no way parallel to my own childhood. This story is fictional with fictional characters and events that I conjured up in my mind. Although we weren't much like the "Brady Bunch" but rather more like "Lost in Space," I did grow up in a happy household, but with my share of accidents, though. I once fell 12 feet from the top of a Silo when I was only 5 years old, and landed on my head against a solid steel pipe. As I staggered home my 16 year old big brother was driving out of our driveway and made a hard stop when he noticed my face covered with blood. I remember him jumping out of the car and scooping me up and carrying me back to the house, shouting to my parents that I was hurt!

Then, about a year later when my mom was driving my middle brother and I home from school, I decided to see what would happen if I pulled the door latch on the back seat door while my mom was taking the turn onto our street. In those days there were no seat belts and I went flying out of the car, and my poor hysterical mom didn't know what to do and just kept driving away! My brilliant middle brother suggested to her that she should probably turn the car around and go back and pick me up. Those incidents revealed my curious adolescent mind, and through my injuries I had acquired great knowledge, the hard way. I learned that gravity can be a real bitch, and for every action there is an equal and opposite reaction. But also that my brothers loved me and wanted to keep me around.

We watched a lot of television in those days, even though we only had 3 channels.

I was a big fan of the 1960's television show "Leave it to Beaver." I always wished for a brother like Wally, but always felt that I was stuck with Eddie Haskel. I'm sure my brother would rebut and say that he wished he had a little brother like Beaver and got stuck with Dennis the Menace, and so the story goes....

Chapter 1

Four AM was a world away for me as a child, but for my father it was routine to be awake and heading over to the dairy barn as we slept. It was arduous work, but a labor of love.

Our dairy farm located in Binghamton, New York had been in our family for over four generations and it was the only life my father knew.

It was the summer of 1945 and my family consisted of my mother and father, my two older brothers, Georgie and Lenny, and me, Sonny.

Georgie and Lenny were three years apart and I was six years younger than my middle brother, Lenny. But often, I felt that even though I was the youngest, I was more mature than the both of them combined.

My brother's chores were that they were required to help out on the farm as much as possible, especially during the summertime. That's what my father expected of them, and no less.

Lenny however, never had it in him to be a farmer and was lazy and always loafing around. Mostly complaining about how much he hated farm work.

My father was constantly chastising and ridiculing Lenny, and he was always yelling and complaining about him.

Lenny couldn't do anything right in my fathers eyes, and he would ride him hard in the hopes that he could someday turn him around, and make a real farmer out of him, which unfortunately only fueled Lenny's total disdain for farming, and my father.

Being the youngest, I was too small to tend to the cattle or do farm chores, so I stayed close to the house and mostly played by myself.

Sometimes I would wander over to the barn and feed the calves and other small animals, but only under my parents or Georgies strict supervision.

The barnyard could be a very treacherous place. The dangerous farming machinery and very aggressive animals made it that way.

Our farm equipment was antiquated, crude and had no safety provisions. Most were designed with sharp blades and powerful chopping teeth, any of which could shear off a hand or finger in a split second if you weren't careful.

A neighboring farmer, who sometimes visits my father, lost half of his arm at the elbow due to a horrific farming accident.

While hay baling a field, he ignorantly reached his arm into the mouth of his hay baler to dislodge a hefty tree branch. The machine's intake grapplers had inadvertently taken hold of the fallen limb, and jammed it up into the machine, locking up the shearing mechanism.

The farmer recklessly left the baler running and didn't anticipate the massive spring-loaded cutting bar releasing as he reached his arm inside the machine to remove the branch.

Tragically, before he could react, his arm was instantly severed and packed into a bale of hay! He managed to wrap a tourniquet made out of baling twine around his amputated stub, and calmly drove the tractor back to the farm where he humorously notified his wife that he had to go to the hospital, and that he may need a few stitches.

It's a sickening freak show at the livestock auctions too.

It's where you can encounter many of the old timers gathering outside the cattle pens, conversing and detailing their horrific farming tales.

They pinch their smoldering Lucky Strike cigarettes between whatever fingers they had left, as they hobble about on their crooked canes, and their disfigured bodies, missing appendages and nasty gaping scars, primarily due to farm machinery and livestock catastrophes.

The huge ferocious breeding bulls my dad kept in a heavily reinforced steel holding pen were also extremely dangerous, and we were always warned to stay far enough away from them.

Although they were much worse during the breeding season, when our cows were in heat and constantly backing up to their enclosures teasing the bulls to mate.

They were a malicious bunch, and without a doubt it was well known that they certainly hated humans more than anything, and they would always relish an opportunity to strike out or gouge a deadly horn whenever possible.

There was another animal even more loathsome and detrimental than the bulls on our farm.

However this beast walked on two legs and it was vicious.

It was my brother Lenny.

He was hardly "Brother of the year," and his tendency was to be physically and mentally abusive towards me, whenever he had the opportunity.

"The day you were born was the worst day of my life, Sonny boy," he would always jeer and scowl.

Then he would punch me in the stomach and throw me on the ground. Sometimes he would even pin me down and strangle me with his bare hands around my throat, but let go just in time, before I passed out and died.

He was always careful though, not to leave any marks that would incriminate himself.

I suppose he resented me because I took the attention away from him when he was exclusively the baby of the family.

Whatever it was, he despised me.

My oldest brother, Georgie, on the other hand was very good to me, and made sure to take time to play with me and he took me places.

One of my favorite things was to go riding with him on his big brown horse, Sarg.

He would bend down and pull me up by my arm and drop me into the saddle right in front of him. I'll never forget the smell of horse sweat and leather, and the creaking sound the saddle made as the horse moved on.

I would hold onto the saddle horn for dear life, and away we would gallop off!

I was never afraid when I was with Georgie, of anything.

The only time I ever had any peace from Lenny was when Georgie was home.

He made sure to take care of things if he ever caught Lenny being aggressive or harsh towards me.

However, Georgie and Lenny also despised each other, and Georgie would take advantage of any opportunity he could to give Lenny a licking too.

It was an unfortunate situation, and it seemed to never end, and it was a vicious circle.

Georgie bullied Lenny and Lenny bullied me.

I was in constant fear of Lenny. Lenny was afraid of Georgie, and we were all afraid of my father.

That's the way we grew up… Afraid.

Chapter 2

When summer had finally ended and school was back in session, my father had to rely more on the hired hands who worked on the farm.

These men were specifically hired to help my father with milking the cows and the usual barn chores, but they were mostly degenerates and sociopaths that could not find work elsewhere, and they were basically the bottom of the barrel as far as hired help was concerned.

Sorry, no cowboy hero's here.

My poor mother had the daunting task of traveling to New York City every few weeks to wrangle up more vagrants to help out on the farm.

She may as well have waited outside of the notorious Rikers Island jail or the psychiatric prison ward of Bellevue hospital for the dischargee's to bring back to the farm.

Basically, if you could walk, carry a bucket and shovel cow manure you were qualified to work.

It didn't matter that you were deviant or a criminal, that's how desperate my parents were for help with the cows.

Sometimes the men would stay on the farm for a few days or even several weeks at a time, until they ran off or they were picked up by the police on outstanding arrest warrants or other criminal activity that they were engaging in.

One of our hired hands in particular, named Eddie, was a very hard worker. There was only one little problem with Eddie... he was a psychopathic sex offender.

A bonified, signed, sealed and registered sexual basket case, pervert!

Oddly, one Saturday afternoon, just after lunch. My brother Georgie heard a strange noise outside the house that sounded as if one of our sheep was in distress.

He looked out the living room window and there was Eddie, naked as a jaybird chasing a ewe around the barnyard!

We laughed hysterically as we watched my mother run out of the house, broom in hand, as she swatted him back into the barn.

You would have thought that would have been enough for my parents to send Eddie packing, but my father desperately needed his help and he had no other choice but to put up with him and his deranged behavior.

"So Eddie had a little problem… At least he wasn't dangerous," so my parents thought.

After that episode with the sheep, Eddie agreed to get some "psychiatric help," and that seemed to put my parents at ease a bit, that at least he was getting some form of treatment for his problem.

However, mental health care then wasn't what it is today, and no one really knew if it would do him any good.

But he was actually behaving, and it seemed to be working.

I don't know how many times he saw the shrink, but what happened next was inevitable.

One Sunday morning, just after brunch, I watched my father from our front porch as he left the house.

He was on his way across the barn yard to the milk room, which was adjacent to the cow barn.

The milk room was basically a small concrete block building which housed two large refrigerators that kept the large cans of milk cool until the transport truck would arrive. It would come several times a week to pick up the milk, and take it to the dairy processing plant.

I don't know if it was the way the sun's beam was casting down upon him or the way he moved, but I thought to myself;

"Holy crap, my dad is big!"

Not fat big, but like John Wayne big!

When my father entered the milk room, he found Eddie completely naked and on all fours "Mooing" and pretending to be a cow and Lenny was "milking" him!

Eddie quickly scrambled up and shoved Lenny at my father, as he hastily raced out of the milk room naked, and hid somewhere in the cow barn!

My father grabbed Lenny and threw him on the ground.

It didn't matter that Lenny was a victim of this sick freak!

All he knew was that it was revolting to him, and Lenny who was thirteen should have known better.

Lenny ran off across the barnyard, pretending to be bawling his eyes out, and hid in an old junk truck that was parked next to the chicken coop, where he instantly stopped his wailing and only started up again when he thought he heard someone was coming and they were going to find him there.

His head bobbed up and down as he looked out for my father.

I watched on as my father followed Eddie's course back into the cow barn.

Calmly but with strong determination he headed into the barn, and he securely closed the flimsy wooden barn door behind him.

It was quiet for a few moments, then suddenly there was a loud explosion of wood bursting apart as Eddy was catapulted and crashed through the barn door by way of my dad's fist!

The door was completely obliterated and only hanging on by one hinge as my father proceeded to beat the living shit out of Eddie, only stopping when he believed Eddie was near dead!

There was so much blood on Eddie's face it was difficult to determine who or what he was!

My father then dragged his naked body by his limp arm across the barnyard toward the bull pen, and effortlessly picked him up, and threw him over the rail into the soggy manure-ridden enclosure as if he were a rag doll, and then left it to the bulls to finish him off.

In a matter of seconds the beasts honed in on him, and began snorting and pawing their enormous hooves in rage! Then they took turns viciously charging and goring him with their razor sharp horns, as they trampled him into the deep wet manure!

My father walked back to the house wiping the blood off his bruised hands with a handkerchief that he pulled out of his back pocket, and he winked at me as I stood there paralyzed on the front porch.

I listened intently through the front door as I overheard him call the police.

He reported that his careless hired hand had been attacked by the bulls as he slipped and fell into their pen.

A few minutes later, all sorts of police cars and even an ambulance quickly arrived at the farm!

Ultimately, Eddie was obviously dead, but no one was willing to go into the bullpen to pull his mangled body out of the muck.

A police officer used a long piece of rope and fabricated a noose. He threw it several times and finally managed to get it around Eddie's bare foot that was sticking up from the slurry of manure, and that's how they dragged him out of the pen.

It was impossible to identify which bull exactly did Eddy in, since they all had blood all over their horns, and so his death was labeled as a farm accident.

The police didn't really seem to care too much, since they all knew about Eddie and his perverted ways.

In fact they were actually joking that Eddie should have probably stuck to chasing the sheep around, and left the bulls alone.

It was never quite the same between Lenny and my father after that day. How could it be?

Chapter 3

As my two brothers got older, they took on more of an active role at the farm. Georgie, being the oldest, was expected to be first in line to inherit the farm when my father retired or died, "Whichever comes first" my father used to say.

Georgie would constantly rib Lenny and jab him that he "might" give him a job cleaning out the pig pen after *he* gets the farm.

As you could imagine that kind of talk didn't go over well with Lenny and his reply would be;

"That's if *you* live long enough to get it, Georgie."

As Lenny got older, he was becoming even more antagonistic and he was more confrontational with everyone and everything around him. He was maniacal and fascinated with killing.

If he ever came across an injured animal, he would relish the opportunity to attack and murder it.

"I'm just doing God's work and putting the poor thing out of its misery," he would sarcastically say.

I actually once saw him chasing after a hobbling kitten with his baseball bat. She seemed to have a thorn stuck in her paw. Before I could stop him, he caught the kitten, and then threw her up in the air and hit her as hard as he could with his baseball bat and shouted "Home run!!"

I ran home crying and told my parents and they always just seemed not to hear me, and would pretend that our family was normal!

He was a sick and very disturbed individual. Maybe worse than Eddie in his own right.

It was bad enough that I had to hide from Lenny at home, but because Lenny had stayed back in fourth and fifth grade, we also attended the same elementary school together, and I was not safe there either.

When I was in the 1st grade, playing with a friend on the playground at school, a group of older kids began bullying us.

Out of the corner of my eye, I noticed my brother Lenny heading our way.

I never thought I would be so happy to see Lenny, charging in to rescue his little brother from the hands of these hoodlums!

"What's going on here?!" he demanded to know.

I desperately pleaded to him;

"These older kids are bullying us, Lenny!"

He paused and his eyes became cross.

"So you big shots want to beat up on my little brother, huh? Well I have something to say about that!" he snarled.

The bullies became nervous and began backing off, for they knew that Lenny was malicious.

Then to everyone's astonishment Lenny stated;

"Good, keep up the good work!" and then he turned his attention back towards me, and he viciously picked me up over his head and threw me to the ground, and then kicked me in the stomach for good measure!

Even the bully's were stunned to see how terrible he was to me!

Lenny then threatened me, and told me that if I ever mentioned this to Georgie, my teacher or our parents, he would strangle me to death while I slept!

I kept my mouth shut, and I choked down my intense pain and tears from my classmates.

Ironically, when recess was over and the bell rang, one of the boys who was bullying us helped me up, and said he was sorry, and that he was glad that he only had a sister at home and not a brother like Lenny.

Chapter 4

Lenny's teenage attitude was getting worse and he was constantly getting into trouble and getting kicked out of school (when he attended). His behavior was spiraling out of control and he was dangerous.

When Lenny finally entered high school, he was the kid you didn't want to piss off.

He was not by far the toughest kid in the school, but if you fought with him, and you gave him a good lickin', you would get some sort of payback, likely in the form of your property vandalized or your pet might just turn up dead.

His usual method of operation was to wait several months before he got even with you, and then just show up at your front door in the middle of the night with a scarecrow sack over his head and his baseball bat in his hands, and clobber you over the head when you open the door.

You never knew what to expect from Lenny, so it was just better to just stay clear of him.

I was very surprised one afternoon when Lenny actually invited me to go along with him, and his friend Eugene to a basketball game at his high school that evening.

I was actually dumbfounded. Why would Lenny want to bring me along?

He never wanted to have anything to do with me, let alone take me anywhere with him.

I hesitated, but I optimistically agreed to go, and later that night, Eugene picked us up in his father's piece of junk Ford station wagon.

Of course I was stuck in the back seat as Lenny was rambling on to Eugene about some cheerleader he liked, and that she was going to be horny for him at the game.

"Hey Eugene, ya know what F.O.R.D stands for? Found. On. Road. Dead!" I chuckled.

"Keep it up wise guy and they just might just find you on the side of the road dead!" Eugene replied.

Lenny turned around and made a disgusting face at me as he ran his finger across his throat, acting in agreement with Eugene. But in hindsight, maybe he wasn't actually acting.

The parking lot was packed with all sorts of cars, trucks and motorcycles but Eugene managed to find a parking place way out in the outer limits, and we had to walk for what seemed forever to get to the gymnasium.

When we finally entered the gym, the crowd was loud and rowdy. We managed to find some seats on the bleachers, but there was only room for two and Lenny and Eugene quickly sat down leaving me to go sit somewhere else by myself.

A pretty high school girl who was sitting behind them noticed that I was looking for a seat and she waved to me, and scooted over so I could sit down next to her. Lenny immediately noticed and gave me a dirty look as I relished the moment.

The game was long and so boring. Lenny and Eugene were completely ignoring me for the most part, but it was nice to be sitting with someone else rather than Lenny, especially a pretty girl who was paying attention to me.

But as I sat there behind them on the bleachers, I noticed a group of several teenage boys intently and maliciously watching Lenny and Eugene.

Actually one boy in particular, was completely focused on giving Lenny an angry death stare.

It was becoming apparent that Lenny wasn't actually there to watch the game, but was rather there only to watch a certain cheerleader named Roxanne, who with her teammates was cheering on the crowd.

He was hopelessly trying to make eye contact with her, and he waved at her whenever he thought she was looking at him.

It was really pathetic listening to him brag to Eugene that she was in love with him.

"She's so hot for me! That girl wants to marry me!" he gloated.

Unfortunately, I didn't see it happening the way he did.

She was obviously sickened by his advances, and she appeared as if she would have rather been shackled and marched up to the gallows of the French Bastille to be guillotined, rather than to have anything to do with Lenny! She was literally trying to avoid making any eye contact with him, and she always hid behind her pom poms whenever she was forced to look in his direction.

The game finally ended and we joined the large crowd which was exiting the building.

We drudged on and continued down a dimly lit sidewalk towards Eugene's car, while Lenny was still carrying on about Roxanne being "So in love with him!" as I lagged several steps behind them.

Suddenly four large boys jumped out from behind the overgrown bushes along the walkway, right in front of Lenny and Eugene and blocked them from going forward!

It was those boys who were watching them at the game.

I recognized one of them, it was Dennis McNearny.

His father owned a massive bolt factory in town, and the family was very well off. Dennis was somewhat of a spoiled rich kid who raced around town in his fancy new red Thunderbird that his father had bought for him when he turned sixteen. And that Cheerleader, the one Lenny was gawking at all night was *his* girlfriend!

They aggressively grabbed Lenny and dragged him off behind the bushes, and pinned him up against the brick wall of the school building.

I just stood there with Eugene, who was reluctant to get involved, and he just cowardly watched as they dragged my brother into the shrubbery.

"Aren't you going to do anything?!! I exclaimed.

"Shut up moron, it's Lenny's love life not mine," he replied.

Dennis began furiously shouting at Lenny, ordering him to stay away from Roxanne!

The other boys pinned Lenny against the wall as Dennis then began brutally punching Lenny in the stomach and face with a pair of brass knuckles that he wore on his fists!

He was beating him so viciously, blood was gushing from his mouth and nose!

As much as I couldn't stand Lenny, he was my brother, and I thought I should do something to help him!

I suddenly noticed a policeman standing at the school's entrance directing the traffic that was leaving and it gave me an idea.

"The Cops are coming!!!" I instinctively shouted.

It was enough to scare the boys into thinking the police were on their way.

They dropped Lenny like a brick, and quickly disappeared into the darkness. Lenny crawled out of the bushes, and Eugene and I rushed over to see if he was conscious.

I tried to help him get up, but he resisted me.

"Get away from me ass wipe!" he shouted at me.

That was the thanks I got for saving his life.

He slowly got himself up and he leaned on Eugene as he hobbled back to the car.

I suddenly realized that Lenny didn't just invite me to the game out of the goodness of his heart, and was being a nice big brother.

No, he knew there was going to be trouble at the game, and he thought they wouldn't bother him if he brought his little brother along.

"Guess you were wrong on that call, Lenny" I thought to myself.

Eugene dropped us off at our house and quickly sped away.

Lenny painfully told me to keep my mouth shut, and he told my parents he had gotten hit in the face by a loose basketball.

Tragically, a few weeks later Dennis McNearny was instantly killed in a horrific car accident.

Apparently someone had removed the "Stop" sign at the intersection at the end of his busy street, and a large furniture delivery truck sped through the intersection and obliterated Dennis's sports car as he was on his way to school that morning!

The police later found the stop sign in the bushes next to the gym, exactly the spot where they beat up Lenny.

No one could ever prove who did it, though. But I knew it had to be Lenny, that was his signature way of getting even.

Days later, Lenny was still chasing after Roxanne, now that Dennis was out of the picture. But she was sickened by him, and tried hopelessly to ignore his advances, especially since everyone believed Lenny had something to do with the accident that killed Dennis.

Finally she told him she would call the police if he continued to bother her. Later that night Lenny poured gasoline all over her cat and strung it up by its neck from a low hanging tree branch in front of her house.

He rang the doorbell and ran away, tossing a match on the cat as he ran past it.

He was really a disturbed teenager, and no one couldn't put anything past him, even killing someone!

Chapter 5

It was Autumn, the day after Halloween, and a brisk Saturday morning. The dew looked like frosting on the grass and things were seemingly quiet on the farm.

I ventured out to the barnyard and I heard voices coming from inside the barn.

It was Lenny and Eugene. They were catching sparrows that were trapped inside the barn's window screens.

One by one, Lenny was carefully placing them in a large rusty bucket which was covered with a small piece of plywood that Eugene was holding down.

"What are you guys doing?" I inquired.

"Get lost, we're saving the sparrows," Lenny rudely replied.

After they gathered about a dozen or so of the little birds, Lenny's demeanor quickly changed and he coyly asked me if I would like to help set them free, outside in the barnyard?

"I would really like that, Lenny! Gee thanks!" I replied.

"Sure Sonny, I guess I've been treating you sort of badly lately, and I'd like to make up for it. Go in the house and get something the birdies would like to eat, because I'm sure they're hungry after being trapped in the barn all night. Then come back here in about 15 minutes, and we'll play a game called "As the sparrows fly," and you can be the one to lift the top off the pail and set them all freeee!" squealed Lenny.

I was so excited! It wasn't often, if ever that Lenny was going out of his way to be nice to me.

I was so thrilled, I ran back to the house and told my mom that Lenny was going to let me set the sparrows free and that I needed some bread for the birds!

She had no idea what I was talking about, but there was a look of concern on her face. I reassured her that everything was going to be okay, as she handed me a stale piece of bread.

"Lenny is in a good mood, and just being nice to me," I assured her.

When I returned back to the barnyard, Lenny was holding the covered bucket with the sparrows inside and patiently waiting for me.

"Okay little brother, when I count to three, hold up the pail and pull the lid off to set the sparrows free!" he jubilantly stated.

"What about the bread I brought for the birds?" I questioned.

"Oh, you can just toss it up in the air. If they are hungry, they can come back for it," he stated.

I was so excited that Lenny was letting me be the one to set the sparrows free, I didn't even care about the bread anymore!

"Onnne…twooo, freeee!" Lenny counted.

I quickly removed the lid, and then Lenny brutally kicked the pail up and out of my hands!

A flurry of birds and feathers were catapulted out of the pail!

But something was terribly wrong!!

Lenny had tied a long stretch of twine to each one of their tiny feeble legs, and they were all tethered together by the single cord!!

They were frantically fluttering and sputtering in all directions as Lenny and Eugene laughed.

The sparrows were frazzled and confused, and they were all tumultuously flipping and spinning out of control on the hard gravel in front of us.

I had to do something! And so, I desperately chased after the storm of flapping feathers! I wanted to help them, and I almost caught hold of the string, until Lenny suddenly grabbed the back of my shirt collar, and pulled me back! Then he wrapped his arm around my throat, putting me in a choke hold, and forced me to watch the distressed little birds as they frantically flailed about!

Miraculously, one of the larger birds caught some wind and was able to get up off the ground and fly upwards. That single sparrow, through sheer determination, was able to lift up off the ground and take flight, and in doing so, he began lifting all the others with him!

Once off the ground, there were some other sparrows that were also able to catch air and also fly upwards! They were lifting the unfortunate other sparrows whose wings were hopelessly tangled up in the cord and were carrying them off with them.

They managed to chaotically rise up above our farm house, jerking each other in all directions until they tragically shifted over and became entangled way up in the high branches of the large sycamore tree next to our porch.

I cried, and with all my strength I broke free from Lenny!

I screamed as loud as I could to get help for those poor little sparrows, but there was nothing anyone could do!

Those poor little birds were entangled high up in the branches, with no chance of escape.

I ran as fast as I could over to the base of the sycamore tree, and hopelessly attempted to climb up it!

That's when I heard the banging sound of someone firing a gun! To my horror, I looked back and saw that it was Lenny, and he was standing there laughing and shooting away up at the entangled sparrows with his 22 semi automatic rifle! I ran over and tried to tackle him, but he aggressively threw me to the ground, and sat on me as he continued shooting at the birds, until he managed to kill them all in a matter of a minute!

Lenny finally got off me, as I was struggling to get up. I wiped the dirt from my teary eyed face, and I noticed Eugene standing there, seemingly mortified as well.

Maybe he didn't completely understand what he was getting into with my psychotic brother, Lenny.

As I ran towards the house to tell my mother, I heard Lenny shout from behind me.

"Thanks for helping me set the birds FREE, Sonny boy! Now that makes you an accomplice to murder!" he jeered.

I ran up the porch steps and into the house crying, I wanted to tell my mother what had happened, and all she could say was;

"Just stay away from Lenny."

For years to come, the twine dilapidated, and the poor decaying sparrows were still visible, tangled high up in that sycamore tree.

It was a horrible day that I will never forget, and I will never forgive my brother for what he did to those poor innocent sparrows.

Chapter 6

The dark age is coming.

Georgie was turning eighteen this coming summer, and planning on going away to college in the fall.

I was mortified, since that would mean that if Georgie was gone, I was in big trouble.

Without Georgie around to safeguard me from Lenny, I was doomed.

I had a little time to figure things out, but Lenny was jealous of the attention Georgie was getting about going off to college, and conflict was really escalating between my two brothers.

In one aspect Lenny was happy to see Georgie go. Why wouldn't he be? His nemesis will be gone, and he will be able to torment me with impunity. But on the other hand, he was jealous of Georgie leaving home and having the freedom of getting the hell off the farm.

Worst of all, with Georgie gone, his workload on the farm would double, and my father would constantly be on his ass, now more than ever.

He also felt that going off to college made my parents proud of Georgie, while Lenny was the disappointment in the family, and the stupid lazy son who never accomplished anything.

Georgie on the other hand was very excited to start his new adventure.

He had been working two jobs pumping gas at two separate gas stations to save up money for a car, and to pay for college.

Our farm was doing okay, but there was no way my parents could afford things like buying cars and paying for school.

That was going to be on us.

Tragically, one night, Georgie came home after work with a pocket full of money.

He went right down into the cellar where he kept his little money safe, secretly hidden.

About a minute later, he frantically came racing up the stairs from the cellar and into the living room where I was watching TV!

He was in a state of panic and tearing the house apart searching for something!

"Hey Sonny, did you happen to see my little money safe?!" he desperately questioned.

His face was all red and sweaty and he was trembling.

"No, what's going on?" I asked.

"My money safe, with all the money that I saved is missing from my hiding spot in the cellar!" Georgie cried.

Just then Lenny came strolling into the room with a sick smile on his face.

"What's going on brothers?" he snickered.

"My money safe is missing! Where is it Lenny!" Georgie demanded.

It was obvious that Georgie was going to accuse Lenny, considering he was the only one in the house who would have done such a thing.

"Maybe it's upstairs somewhere. Did you check Sonny's closet?" Lenny dumbfoundly suggested.

"*My closet*?!!" I shouted.

Georgie then instantly darted up the stairs to our bedroom, and began searching through the room which Lenny and I tragically shared.

I followed quickly behind him while Lenny leisurely made his way up the stairs after us.

Georgie began recklessly tearing through Lenny's closet, and then ransacked his bureau and bed! But nothing turned up.

"I'm really offended! Why does everyone always blame me for everything that goes sour around here? I bet Sonny took your money, because he doesn't want you to leave him alone with me while you go off to college! In fact just this afternoon I saw him down at the drug store after school with a bunch of kids. He was buying them all ice cream cones and loads of candy! Sonny boy took your money, because he doesn't want you to leave home!" spewed Lenny.

I was so taken aback, I couldn't even breath!

Georgie walked over to me, and sat me down on my bed.

"I know you wouldn't take my money, Sonny. But look for it, if you find it, I'll give you a reward!" Georgie directly stated to me.

I knew what that meant...If you took it, I'll give you a chance to give it back!

"Georgie, honestly, I didn't take your money! I would never do that to you!" I cried.

Lenny then marched over to my bed and ruffled up the sheets and looked under my pillow as if he was doing Georgie a favor and helping him look for his money.

Then he went to my closet, and he began tossing my things out onto the floor.

Suddenly he froze as if in disbelief as he stopped fumbling through my things.

"Oh yeah, then what's this, Sonny?!" jeered Lenny.

He turned towards us and revealed Georgie's little tin safe which was now demolished, and the door was smashed open.

Lenny cynically lifted the safe, opened the mutilated little door and peeked inside, then discouragingly shook his head and then tried to empty its contents by shaking it sideways. A lonely five dollar bill gently floated out of it, and landed on the floor.

"Hmmm, only $5 dollars left from over $750.00. You must have bought a lot of ice cream cones for your pals Sonny!" jeered Lenny as he was relishing the moment.

I got all choked up and started crying hysterically! I didn't know what else to do!

Georgie walked over to me and put his hand on my shoulder.

"It's okay Sonny boy, I know you didn't take my money. Now run along out to the barn, and make sure I locked up the chicken coop," Georgie stated.

I didn't know if it was a trick, or if he really believed me!

I was somewhat relieved, but I didn't understand why he wanted me to get out of the house.

The chicken coop had a spring door, it doesn't have a lock on it.

He then let go of me, nodded at me to leave, and waited by the door as I left the room.

Then he clenched his fists and turned his attention toward Lenny.

Lenny could see by the angry dead-eyed stare that Georgie had planted on him, that he was in big trouble.

Desperately, Lenny began shaking and he tried to flip Georgies attention back on me.

"It was Sonny Boy!!!! Sonny boy took your money!!!" shouted Lenny.

"Oh Yeah, scumbag?! Then how did you know there was more than $750.00 in the safe? I never told anyone how much money I had!" shouted Georgie.

It was a mistake that Lenny would live to regret.

Lenny tried to make a run for it out the door, but Georgie was there blocking his escape!

I ran out of the house and hid in the barn. From there, I could hear Georgie beating the living shit out of Lenny.

My parents were gone, visiting a neighbor that night, and without any knowledge of what was happening at home.

Lenny did finally manage to break free of Georgie's wrath, and he crashed through the second floor window onto a briar bush below.

He was a bloody mess as he limped off, disappearing into the darkness of the night.

Chapter 7

The following morning was eerily quiet on the farm.

My mother was cutting carrots for a stew, and was concerned that Lenny had not been home all night and she asked me if I had seen him when I came down for breakfast.

"Nope," was my reply, and I sat down and began eating my pancakes.

My father was heading back out to the barn, and he asked me about the broken window in my room?

"Lenny did it," I replied.

My mother continued cutting up carrots, and I asked her if it would be okay if I could give some of the peels to Sarg, Georgie's horse.

She stuffed the carrot scraps into a brown paper bag, and I ventured out to the meadow where Sarg was always out grazing.

When I saw him in the distance, he was standing under the old apple tree on the other side of the meadow.

Oddly, he appeared smaller than usual, and he was carrying himself awkwardly.

I called out to him, but he just stood there motionless, and refused to move.

As I approached him, I sensed something was very wrong with him.

His grand stature was diminished and he looked sunken and feeble, and his head was hung low.

My walk turned into a run as my heart began to pound, and I began to race toward him!

I could see he was not right, and there was something terribly wrong with Sarge's front leg.

When I finally got close enough, I saw that his front leg was totally broken in two, and there was a large bloody gaping wound across his forehead and dried blood all over his face!

His leg was grotesquely dangling there, snapped in two below the knee, and next to him, there was a blood stained hickory axe that was driven in the crotch of the old apple tree.

It was obviously left there on purpose, a message that this was not an accident, but rather an act of vengeance.

I knew it was a serious injury and I had to get help, and I was sick to my stomach with fear and I ran as fast as I could, back to the farm to get my father!

He was in the barn, struggling to pull a breech calf from a cow when I stormed in and he was surprised to see me, but knew right away that something was terribly wrong!

With a final tug he yanked the calf free and quickly approached me.

"What's going on?!!" he impatiently shouted.

I was so upset and out of breath that I couldn't speak!!

He started to shake me and asked me again what was wrong!

All I could utter out was;

"Sarg...Sarg is in a bad way!!"

My father immediately ran into the house, and grabbed his Winchester rifle from the gun rack hanging over the fireplace, and commanded me to stay home as he ran past me in the barnyard.

He raced out to Sarg's meadow as fast as I had ever seen him run!

I cried hysterically as I ran into the house and told my mother what had happened.

Georgie heard the ruckus and came running down the stairs!

"What's going on?!!" he shouted.

I couldn't tell him. I just continued sobbing and holding onto my mom.

"There's been an accident, Georgie...Sarg is hurt," mom calmly stated.

Georgie instantly panicked and ran out of the house, and that's when we heard the gunshot!

The loud "Bang!" echoed across our farm like a random strike of lightning with its crackling, booming thunderclap. And we all froze in dreadful silence.

"No! No! Nooo!!!" shrieked Georgie.

"Please Lord, not Sarg!!" he cried out.

He frantically ran towards Sarg's meadow.

Thrashing aimlessly through the tall green meadow grass, until he finally arrived at the place where his horse had spent its agonizing night.

There under the apple tree, whose morning shade blanketed him for his final moment, laid Sarg...dead.

My father was actually teared up and leaning over Sarg's twitching body, making sure he was out of his misery when Georgie arrived.

"I'm sorry, Son, he had to be put out of his misery. His leg was broken and his skull was smashed in. I don't know how he made it through the night," my father sadly spoke.

Georgie was overwhelmed with grief and fell upon Sarg, sobbing.

My father took him by the arm and tried to pull him away, but he resisted.

"Come on, Son. Let's go home," requested my father.

Georgie finally found what little bit of strength he had left and slowly stood up.

They walked back together with their heads down low and my father's arm was around Georgies shoulder, as he helped him stagger back to the house.

"Where's Lenny?!!" demanded my father as they entered the house.

No one had seen him since he ran away from home last night.

However, the old farm truck was missing, and we knew Lenny must have had something to do with it.

Later that afternoon, my father received a phone call from the state police. They caught Lenny attempting to rob a gas station about 60 miles away in Ithaca.

He assaulted an elderly gas station attendant with a tire iron, and then robbed the cash register.

Unlucky for Lenny, an off duty police officer just happened to pull up at the same time, and he easily apprehended Lenny.

He noted that Lenny looked as if he had been badly beaten and ran through a blood bath, but it was someone else that had given him that lickin', and not the police.

My father sternly glanced at Georgie, and noticed that his hands and knuckles were badly bruised.

The officer continued on and asked if my father was prepared to post bail for his son, Leonard.

My father unsympathetically replied to the officer that;

"He had no son named Leonard," and hung up the phone.

My mother became hysterical and started screaming!

Nevertheless, she knew my father was right.

Lenny was a bad seed from the start, and it was time that he had to start figuring things out for himself.

Besides, no one could ever forgive what he had just done to poor innocent Sarg.

The court found Lenny guilty, and sent him upstate to the New York State School for Delinquent Boys, which was actually supposed to be a reform school.

Since Lenny was only 16 and not yet an adult, that's where he ended up. Several times Lenny had called my mother and father, begging them to get him out of there.

He promised to be good, but my father had nothing to say to him and just hung up the phone.

The "Reform school" was supposed to be a place that would rehabilitate Lenny, and help him see the light and change his devious ways.

But instead, the environment there only made him worse, and educated him to become even more of a degenerate, if that was possible.

He quickly made himself at home in prison, and felt comfortable being with other delinquents like himself, although he was considered the worst of the bunch.

He quickly formed an entourage of younger boys who actually looked up to Lenny. Even though he bullied them into doing his dirty work at the detention center, they were ignorant and impressed with his corrupt and evil ways.

He served there for two years before they had to release him, due to the law at the time which stated that;

"When a juvenile turned eighteen, they were no longer considered a juvenile and his record would be sealed and they would be released. Unless they were convicted as an adult."

However, those two years festered in Lenny's mind, and he was angry that his family had turned their backs on him.

With no other place to go, he called a boy he befriended from the reform school.

He had just been released a few months prior, and he lived in New York City. His name was Joey Calderone.

Joey was a tall, gangly seventeen year old boy, who had been trying to grow a mustache since he was thirteen.

It seemed that Lenny and Joey had a lot in common. They both were degenerates that blamed everyone else for their problems, and they both were criminals, looking for opportunity.

Joey had been arrested for stealing a woman's Mercedes which was parked near Central park. He was tipped off that it was left there with the keys in the ignition. If that wasn't bad enough, he wound up crashing the stolen car into a police cruiser that was parked outside of the police station, as he was being pursued by another police car.

They didn't have very far to go to throw him in jail.

His stepfather, Big Al was a high level mob boss that ruled New York City with an iron fist and was loan sharking, booking and selling "insurance" to the merchants of Little Italy, Chinatown and the rest of the city.

Joey had mentioned to Lenny that when he got out of "Juvie" to call him, he would introduce him to his step dad, who would likely give him a job working for the mob. That was really appealing to Lenny since he felt that might just be something he could be good at...being a mobster.

Joey was excited when he heard from Lenny, and they made arrangements to meet up at Grand Central station, in New York City.

On the afternoon of his eighteenth birthday, Lenny was marched out to the entrance of the detention center, and was literally picked up and thrown through the air, out of the main gate by several of the guards, who then heckled him with the nickname they had appropriately conjured up for him during his stay there, "Listeria Lenny." The sinister bacterium that infects humans through contaminated food.

He proudly got up off the ground and brushed himself off, and then threw the guards both middle fingers as he took a deep breath of his newfound freedom.

He made his way down the long prison driveway to the road, and hitch hiked his way to the local train station with only a few dollars in his pocket and the clothes on his back.

Unfortunately, he didn't have enough money for the train fare, but he managed to rob an old crippled man on crutches in the station's restroom.

He viciously hit the old man over the head with the restroom garbage can, dazing him and knocking him unconscious as he came out of the toilet stall.

Then he pushed him back onto the toilet and punched him a few more times until the man fell over onto the floor. He took the old man's watch, then groped through the man's pockets and took his wallet.

When Lenny finally boarded the train, he noticed several policemen rushing past him towards the restroom.

He chuckled with no remorse, pondering how easy it was to rip off that old crippled man, as he admired his new watch.

Chapter 8

Joey had been impatiently waiting around for Lenny to arrive at the train station, and he was picking a few pockets to pass the time.

It was just past 9 PM when his train finally rolled into Grand Central station. Lenny was getting nervous that maybe Joey was just all talk and had no intention of showing up, let alone introducing him to his mobster stepfather.

He cautiously got off the train, and followed the other passengers up the stairs to the main lobby of Grand Central station.

The gigantic lobby was magnificent to him, especially since he had never ventured very far outside of Binghamton, except for the reform school.

This was the first time he was in a big city, and he liked it.

Suddenly felt someone's hand reaching into his back pocket, lifting his wallet and he quickly jerked and spun around with his fist pulled back, ready to strike.

"Gotcha sucker!" Joey chuckled.

"Screw you, ya moron!" Lenny laughed and was relieved that it was Joey pulling his leg and that he actually showed up!

They both seemed happy to see each other, and they almost hugged before Lenny pulled away.

As they left the station, they joked and bumped into each other jovially and marched onward toward Joey's car, which was parked in a dark nearby alley.

It was a brand new white Corvette convertible.

"Holy crap, Joey! Nice car!" exclaimed Lenny.

"Yeah, I just picked it up... it's sort of a loaner, get in!" chuckled Joey.

"Wow, this must have set you back a few bucks!" declared Lenny.

"Naa, let's just say I picked it up when nobody was looking, if ya know what I mean!" Joey sarcastically stated.

The two boys laughed as Joey fumbled with a pair of loose wires from underneath the driver's side dashboard. A few electrical sparks could be heard, and then the car's engine hesitated a few seconds but then Joey got it started, and they raced off in the stolen Corvette.

They were now on their way to Little Italy to meet up with Joey's step father, Big Al.

Little Italy in the late 1950's was a dangerous place.

If you didn't have mob protection you needed protection from the mob.

Joey recklessly parked his car in a narrow alley, purposely running into a row of garbage cans, clearing them out of the way to make room for his car.

The boys then hopped out, and began briskly walking down the busy streets of Little Italy, with Joey leading the way.

Oddly, the merchants and restaurateurs on the sidewalks were randomly shouting out compliments to Joey!

"Yo Joey, lookin' good! Please send my respect to Big Al!" was the norm.

"Wow, you're really popular around here!" remarked Lenny.

"Yeah, it's because of my step dad. Nobody wants their legs broken for disrespecting the boss. They basically all know my step dad doesn't give a shit about me, but just in case, they brown nose me. I guess they think someday I might take things over from the old son of a bitch. 'With fear you get respect,' that's what my stepdad always says," proclaimed Joey.

Chapter 9

The boys finally arrived at a quaint Italian restaurant, which was set between a massage parlor and a small Italian grocery market.

Its large red, white and green neon sign flickered and buzzed, and it was obviously much larger than all of the other signs in Little Italy.

It was called "Castel Buono" and it was owned by Big Al, himself.

When they entered the restaurant Lenny instantly noticed that everything inside was the color red.

The carpet, the wallpaper, even the chairs and table cloths were red.

The walls were decorated with dozens of pictures of the Castle Buono, which was located in Sicily along with other iconic Italian and Sicilian sites.

And that night, the restaurant was particularly crowded, loud and noisy.

An elderly Italian waiter noticed Joey, and quietly escorted them to the back, where there was a special secluded area, where Joey's stepfather and two other large thugs were eating, drinking and carrying on.

As Joey approached their table, Big Al noticed him and his face grew contorted with a look of disgust, and he threw his knife and fork down on the table!

"If it isn't da idiot son o ma wife. Did yaz have to show up and ruin my dinner?" he jeered.

Joey seemed to shrug it off in a manner that he was accustomed to.

"So Dad, this is the kid I told you about that I met in the joint, his name is Lenny," remarked Joey.

"Please! I thought I told youz never to call me that! You have a loser of a real daddy. The one that bounced you on his knee. I'm the guy who's going to bounce you off my foot!" scolded Big Al, and the two thugs began laughing.

Al was a large, heavy set Sicilian mobster with a strong Italian accent.

His cloth napkin was tucked into his shirt collar, and it was heavily soiled with tomato sauce and olive oil.

"And by da way, you were in a pissy reform school big shot, not da joint!" sarcastically stated Big Al.

The two men that were seated with him once again burst out laughing hysterically.

It seemed that the street merchants weren't the only ones sucking up to Big Al. The two thugs were so patronizing that their loud laughter could be heard throughout the restaurant.

"So Lonny, you want to be a made man?" joked Big Al.

"His name is Lenny," replied Joey sternly.

"Lonny, Lenny what's the difference? Anyway, you seem to me to be a dip shit kid. Why should I give you a shot working for me?" taunted Big Al.

Lenny was caught off guard and began to stutter.

"Well I,I,I.." stuttered Lenny.

"What's da matter, big shot? Can't yaz talk?! The last thing I need is a stoonade like my step idiot here, messing things up for me!" exclaimed Big Al.

42

The two thugs and Big Al began laughing hysterically!

They laughed so boisterously, that their food was falling out of their mouths onto the table.

"Yeah clown, go back to your pee-pee penitentiary!" shouted one of the thugs.

The uproarious laughter escalated, and then in Lenny's mind, everything went silent.

Lenny flashbacked to the farm, reminiscing of the times that his father would demean him, and call him a stupid idiot, a loser and good for nothing.

"Stupid idiot! Loser! Good for nothing!" echoed in his mind.

Lenny sadly gazed down at the floor, clenched his fists, and excused himself to go to the restroom.

"Yeah, go pee pee kid, before you wet your di di diaper!" shouted Big Al, and once again there was an uproar of laughter.

Lenny walked away in shame and kicked the door open into the restroom.

He began punching the walls until his fists were bloody, and then he noticed a broken iron steam pipe hanging from the ceiling.

He grabbed hold of it and angrily began bending it back and forth until it snapped free.

His brain was numb, but filled with rage as he returned back to the table, concealing the steel pipe under his draped coat.

"Oh look the re, re ree-tard returns!" bellowed Big Al, and he and his thugs continued on with their uncontrollable laughter.

"Yeah, I re, ree-turned you fat ass pigs!" Lenny angrily shouted.

Without any hesitation, Lenny dropped his coat and swiftly swung the steel pipe, smashing the two thugs heads like watermelons!

Their skulls cracked wide open as their blood and spaghetti splattered against the walls, as their huge bodies fell out of their chairs and onto the floor!

Big Al scrambled for his gun, which was concealed in a shoulder holster under his jacket, but Lenny delivered a decisive blow to his shoulder, dislocating his arm and his pistol dropped to the floor!

Lenny then mercilessly continued on, bludgeoning the man's head with the steel pipe until his large bloody head collapsed into his plate full of spaghetti, and it was obvious that he was dead.

Lenny was covered with blood splatter and spaghetti, as he dropped the iron steam pipe onto the floor, and he bent over and picked up the large black gun that Big Al had pulled on him.

As Lenny stood back up he aimed the gun at Joey who was in a state of paralysis by what he had just witnessed.

"Wait a minute Lenny!!" Joey shouted.

He scampered toward his stepfather's lifeless body and picked up the steel pipe which Lenny had used to obliterate the man.

Then he raised it over his head and began delivering more and more decisive blows to his lifeless step father's head.

If there was any doubt that Big Al wasn't already dead, he was certainly dead now.

"I hated this piece of garbage!! He treated me and my mom like shit!" exclaimed Joey.

Joey then reached down and pulled out a small brown leather notebook from his stepfather's bloody inside jacket pocket.

"This is our ticket to fortune Lenny! Let's get out of here before the rest of his gang comes looking for us!" exclaimed Joey.

But just before they were about to leave the scene, Joey stopped and pulled a humongous diamond ring off Big Al's bloody finger.

"This ten carat diamond ring he used to call his "Lucky charm," not so lucky today, Daaad," jeered Joey, and he tossed the large gold ring to Lenny.

"Big Al lifted it from a gangster called "Frank the Indian," a rival mob boss that he had rubbed out a few years back. Maybe it's not so lucky after all, it seems whoever is wearing it, sooner or later winds up a dead man," stated Joey.

"Why did they call him 'The Indian'?" Lenny questioned, as he began to regain his composure.

"It was pretty well known that after Frank would knock somebody off, he would scalp 'em' as a trophy. Eventually he had so many hairy scalps that he had a jacket made out of them!" Joey eerily replied.

Lenny made a bewildered face as he placed the large ring on his finger and admired it.

"Does this mean we are married?" Lenny joked.

Joey laughed and Lenny placed Big Al's gun under his belt and they both quickly scampered out the back door.

They disappeared into the darkness of the alley as they heard police sirens approaching from the distance.

When the police finally arrived at the restaurant, it was somewhat of a relief to them that someone had literally whacked Big Al.

He was holding loans and book debt on most of the cops in the area and they figured that since Big Al was dead, so was their debt.

Chapter 10

The boys made their way back to Joey's stolen Corvette and they were both excessively charged up with adrenaline.

Joey was recounting and portraying the entire confrontation over and over, and Lenny was also gloating his version of the story just as any eighteen year old derelict would do.

"That big fat piece of shit had it comin'! When I went to the can, I was pretty pissed off. My old man used to talk to me kinda the same way. 'Loser, stupid idiot, good for nothing' and those words were ringin' in my head! Somethin' came over me and when I saw that pipe hangin' over my head, it looked like it was put there by God himself for me to bash those freakin' ass holes brains in!" Lenny bragged.

"It was the craziest freaking thing I ever saw! While you were gone Big Al was yucking it up about taking us to the dock and using us for fishing bait! Then when you came back, WHAM-O!! Spaghetti and meat heads all over the place!" Joey exclaimed.

"We've gotta get out of town, I figure Big Al's gang will be lookin for us," stated Lenny.

"Yeah, but first we need some cash, and I know where there will be a load of it," replied Joey.

He accelerated the Corvette's engine, and they raced recklessly toward Big Al's secret hideout.

It was located in a run down building near the seedy area of the waterfront.

There was a heavy set thug with dyed jet black hair sitting at a desk in the office, cleaning his gun when Joey and Lenny stormed in.

"Hey! What da hell are you doin' here? Big Al told me to shoot ya if ya ever showed up here, Joey!" the thug sarcastically shouted.

Lenny quickly removed Big Al's pistol from his belt and instantly shot the man directly in the forehead!

The thug was propelled backwards, flipping over out of his seat and was instantly dead.

That was the first time Lenny had ever shot and killed a person, even though he constantly thought about it, he never had the opportunity to actually pick up a gun and do it.

He felt empowered. The loud bang, the force of the gun recoiling in his hand, and the bullet knocking that thug out of his chair.

That gun made him feel like everything he ever wanted to be. Feared and respected.

Joey then scampered over and moved a rug on the floor, and exposed a trap door which led down into a dark room in the basement.

The two boys carefully stepped down a narrow iron spiral staircase, and Joey blindly reached for, and pulled on a chain at the bottom of the stairs to turn on a swinging light bulb that was hanging from the ceiling.

In Big Al's secret office there was an old green metal desk with a matching roller chair, a large iron safe and several gun lockers filled with Thompson machine guns, pistols, and ammunition which was piled up to the ceiling!

Lenny picked up one of the Tommy guns and pointed it at Joey,

"Stick 'em up, wise guy!" he joked.

"Stop messing around with that, and help me find the combination to this safe!" exclaimed Joey.

"My older brother once had a safe, I popped that dinky thing open like a pimple. This one wouldn't be so easy," stated Lenny.

The safe was about the size of an icebox, but made out of solid steel.

The boys searched everywhere as they ransacked the office, but couldn't find the numerical combination to the safe anywhere.

"Hey, what was in that little book you took from Big Al?" questioned Lenny.

"It's a journal with the list of all the loans, bets and protection payments that were run by Big Al," replied Joey.

Lenny took the book and found it to be all encrypted in some sort of code.

The names were clear but numbers seemed to be given an alphabetical letter to correspond to them.

On the last page there it was: Left CA, Right TU, Left AA, Right ES.

They began tearing apart Big Al's desk, hoping to find the answer sheet to decode the book, but found nothing except dirty girly magazines and past due restaurant invoices.

But as they continued looking through Big Al's desk, Joey had found a large manilla envelope with his name printed on it, and his picture enclosed along with the names of the places he frequented.

There were also five one hundred dollar bills in the envelope along with a note which read, "Make it look like an accident!"

"Lenny!! Al was putting a hit on me! That piece of shit was going to have me whacked, and for only 500 bucks! I want to go back there and smash his head in a few more times!" cried Joey.

"Ya don't have to worry about him anymore," stated Lenny as he continued looking for the code.

The diamond ring was loose and falling off his finger.

Lenny took it off and noticed there was some sort of engraving on the inside, and read it out loud;

"My Brother's Keeper"

"What's up with the engraving inside this ring?" questioned Lenny.

"Big Al has two older mobster brothers that live in Chicago. They are really close, and they are going to be really pissed when they find out someone literally "put the hit" on Big Al!" replied Joey.

Just then Lenny noticed a painting on the wall, it was of an old castle.

"What's with that castle? It was plastered all over his restaurant too," inquired Lenny pointing at the artwork.

"That castle is from the town that Big Al and his family came from in Sicily. The name is printed on the brass plate attached to the bottom of the frame 'Castel Buono.'"

I had to listen to that piece of garbage go on and on about his youth there. He told me when he was twelve, it was the first place he ever killed somebody. He threw a kid who owed him something like $15 bucks from that castle tower!" replied Joey as he pointed to the highest point of the tower.

"Lets try something that I once saw on a box of cereal. They had code words made up of numbers," stated Lenny.

He picked up a pencil and wrote the name "Castelbuono" on a sheet of paper.

"These letters are the same as the ones in the book," remarked Lenny. He wrote a #1 under the C, #2 under the A, #3 under the S and continued placing digits all the way to the N where he placed a zero.

C A S T E L B U O N O
1 2 3 4 5 6 7 8 9 0

"But there's another "O" at the end of the name," commented Joey.

"Fugget about it, cheese dip!" replied Lenny.

"Let's try these numbers… CA=12, TU=48, AA=11 and ES=53."

Their hearts pounded with anticipation as Lenny's sweaty fingers began spinning the numbered dial on the large iron safe.

As Lenny approached the last digit, #53, he could feel the final tumbler tighten up and was beginning to drop into position.

"Son of a bitch, it worked!!" Lenny exclaimed.

Just as Lenny began pulling the lock release lever, they heard a tumult and voices upstairs.

It was Big Al's gang of thugs, two of which were the ones that were with Big Al at the restaurant, and there were about six other gang members with them!

"I guess you didn't kill those guys," whispered Joey.

Lenny quickly turned off the light and picked up two Tommy guns from the gun locker, and snapped on a drum full of ammunition onto each of them and chambered the first bullet.

"Yo Joey, is that you down there?" one of the thugs called down.

Joey erratically motioned to Lenny to toss him a gun, as the thugs began to investigate the steps spiraling down to the secret office.

However, Lenny did not comply.

Lenny didn't trust anyone, especially Joey, who could possibly turn on him and keep Big Al's loot all for himself.

Instead he motioned to Joey to be quiet and hide.

One by one, the gangsters hesitantly made their way down the steep spiral staircase, with their guns in hand.

Lenny was hiding next to the safe while Joey was under the desk.

"Yo Joey, it's me Carmine...We just want to talk to ya. Don't worry, me and Sebby ain't mad at ya, we got hurt pretty bad, but we know you had nothin' to do wid it. But we need to talk to your friend. Is "Lonny" wid ya down there? Since Big Al is now dead, you'z the new boss...is that okay with ya, Joey?" sarcastically stated Carmine.

Lenny strongly motioned to Joey to keep quiet!

The men continued to cautiously meander down to the bottom of the spiral stairs.

While standing nervously in the dark, Carmine, still covered in blood and spaghetti sauce, fumbled about as he was searching through the air for the pull chain to turn on the light. His head was heavily bandaged with streaks of blood soaking through, along with his partner Sebby, whose head was similarly bandaged, was right behind him, holding a machine gun and was ready to use it.

"Don't ya think we should spread out?" whispered one of the men as Carmine finally found the pull chain.

Just as Carmine clicked on the light, Lenny sprang out and began firing his machine gun at the men!

Bullets, blood and bone fragments sprayed across the spiral staircase and all over Big Al's map of Sicily.

Lenny's teeth were tightly clenched as the machine gun rhythmically jerked back and forth in his hands, until the bullet drum was finally empty!

The room was full of dense white smoke and even though some of the thugs managed to squeeze off a few shots, Lenny didn't have a scratch on him.

Joey crawled out from underneath the desk and began cheering.

"Holy Shit! That was awesome Lenny!! Lenny the…uhh,...uhh," shouted Joey. Lenny dropped the flaming hot gun and was picking up the other machine gun and chambered a bullet.

Joey suddenly seemed puzzled, why Lenny was reaching for the second gun since all the men were already dead.

"What were ya gonna say, Joey? Lenny the... loser?" angrily stated Lenny.

"Uh no, no Lenny! I was going to say Lenny the...the Assassinator!" pleaded Joey.

Sorry Joey, that don't rhyme! You're the only one who knows my name and that I whacked Big Al and his gang. I can't have a loose screw like you running around town ratting me out," stated Lenny.

Joey desperately raised his hands in an attempt to shield himself, but before he could utter a single word, to save himself, Lenny shot and killed Joey with a rip of bullets.

Lenny then casually picked up a cigarette that was smoldering on the floor and took a deep drag from it.

He slowly swaggered over to the safe, admiring all the men he had just killed as he stepped over Joey's lifeless body.

He took hold of the thick steel lever and pulled it, and it moved freely to the right. He felt the locking bolts slide across the inside of the door releasing its constraint on the door.

Lenny envisioned all sorts of treasures and loot which were possibly going to be inside the safe, and all that treasure was going to be all his, now that Joey was out of the picture.

But at first glance, the safe was just full of important papers, souvenir junk and several stacks of bundled money, totaling about $20,000.

There was a drawer at the bottom of the safe, which contained a very expensive looking hand engraved chrome 45 caliber pistol with white ivory pistol grips.

Also in the drawer was a black and white photograph of Big Al with Frank Sinatra, and another photograph of a thug (who resembled Big Al) in front of a Pizza parlor called "Sedone's of Chicago" which Lenny tossed on the floor.

There was a freakishly shriveled up man's finger in a jar of yellow formaldehyde liquid in the drawer, too.

He presumed it was the finger of "Frank the Indian" who had previously owned the enormous diamond ring that was now on his finger.

He heard one of the men groaning, and thought that he had better get going before any more of Big Al's mobsters showed up.

But first, he casually walked over and located the thug who was still alive and shot him one more time in the head, and then matter of factly returned back to what he was doing.

Lenny had no compassion, empathy or remorse for anyone, and he was enjoying it.

He noticed a crumpled up olive drab duffle bag stuffed in one of the lockers, and immediately tossed in it, a Tommy gun, along with several drums of ammunition, all of Big Al's money and for some unknown reason other than he thought it was cool, "Frank the Indians" grotesque marinated finger.

He also picked up the envelope from the desk which contained the $500 Big Al had left for Joey's hit and stuffed the money in his coat pocket.

He felt that he earned it considering the money was deemed for whoever killed Joey.

Before he left, he once again returned to the safe for a second look over to see if he had missed anything, and then he removed Al's fancy chrome gun out of the drawer and placed it behind his back, under his belt.

As he finally began to leave, he once again noticed the photograph which he had tossed on the floor of Big Al's brother, and his pizza restaurant in Chicago.

"Hmmm, I always wanted to go to Chicago. I just might fit right in there," he thought and he picked up the picture and stuffed it into the sack along with Big Al's journal.

On his way out, he knelt down next to Joey's dead body and patted him on the head.

"Sorry Joey, but remember what I told you back in clink... never trust a scorpion," he whispered.

Then he quickly took off, hopping and climbing over all the dead bodies as he made his way up the spiral stairs, carrying the heavy duffle bag of loot over his shoulder.

As he began to exit the building, he peeked outside to see if any other mobsters might be hiding and waiting for him, and then he nonchalantly walked out of the building, and quickly disappeared into the dreary alleyways of the New York City waterfront, and returned to Joey's hot wired stolen Corvette. After a few tries he managed to start the engine and was off in search of the train station, and looking to hop on to the first train out of the city to Chicago.

Chapter 11

It was just about midnight before Lenny finally stumbled upon the train station.

Unfamiliar with the city, he drove around in circles until he noticed a police officer standing in the middle of 5th avenue directing traffic, and he nervously asked him for directions.

When he finally arrived at the train station, he simply stopped the car right in the middle of 34th Street, got out of the car with his duffle bag, and carelessly left the car running with the door wide open in the middle of the street, and he walked away and never looked back.

He lugged the heavy duffle bag over his shoulder into the train station, and approached the ticket counter.

There was a sour old shell of a man sitting at the counter, surrounded by a thick glass enclosure.

He was reading a book, and it was apparent that the last thing he wanted was to be disturbed by some unfortunate patron in need of a train ticket.

It was obvious that he hated his job, and was fed up with the grind of dealing with rude smelly people all day long.

All he really wanted was to be left alone, finish his shift, and go home to his aquarium fish, who were trapped inside a glass container just like himself.

It was the late shift, and there was no one in line to buy tickets.

Lenny marched right up to the ticket window and dropped his duffle bag on the floor behind him.

The ticket master who was protected behind a large panel of thick glass ignored him, and continued on reading his book.

Lenny became impatient and made a grunting noise and rapped Big Al's diamond ring on the window to get his attention.

"Hey, bookworm!! When's the next train outa here to Chicago?" Lenny rudely barked at the attendant.

Slowly and reluctantly the man put down his book and looked over the top of his glasses at Lenny.

"Next train out is the 12:35 Excelsior to Chicago... Twelve dollars one way. Twenty dollars round trip," replied the attendant.

"I'll take it one way," replied Lenny.

Lenny then reached into his jacket pocket and removed a one hundred dollar bill.

He purposely crumpled it up into a ball, and tossed it through the semi circular hole at the base of the glass window at the attendant.

The ticket master gave Lenny a dirty look, but took the money and slowly unfolded it.

As the attendant began working on the ticket, Lenny suddenly noticed the strong fragrance of a women's cheap perfume.

When he turned to identify its source, there was a tall, scantily clad, sleazy white woman standing several feet away from him, near the ticket counter.

She was obviously a prostitute, wearing a tight mini skirt, a braless halter top and a blond wig. Her face was layered with gobs of makeup along with extra long false black eyelashes and bright red lipstick.

When she saw that Lenny had noticed her, she purposely turned away and spilled the contents of her purse onto the floor, and proceeded to hike up her tiny skirt so that she could lewdly bend over at the hip and pick up her things from the floor.

As she seductively bent over, Lenny quickly realized that the woman was not wearing any underwear whatsoever, and that she was enticing him by revealing her goods to him!

Lenny kinked his neck and dipped his head down to get a better view, as she slowly gathered her things off the floor, but then suddenly after about a minute she quickly snatched up her remaining items and ran off as if she was going to miss her train.

The ticket master impatiently knocked on the glass partition to regain Lenny's attention, and reciprocated by recklessly crumpling up Lenny's ticket and change into a ball, and he shoved it back under the glass window at Lenny.

"Gate 23, Excelsior departs in 15 minutes," the man scoffed.

Lenny gave the man a cold stare, and just grabbed his ticket and change without saying "Thanks" and recklessly stuffed them into his pocket as he maintained his cold stern eye contact with the ticketmaster.

As he leaned back to reach for his duffle bag, he suddenly realized that there was nothing there!

"Son of a Bitch!! Somebody stole my duffle bag!" he shouted.

Lenny desperately looked in all directions but there was no sign of anyone.

"Where did that whore go?!" Lenny shouted at the ticket master.

The man just smiled and shrugged his shoulders, as he seemed to be enjoying the fact that Lenny had just gotten ripped off.

"The old bait and switch! How could I have fallen for that!" Lenny exclaimed.

As the hooker was distracting him, her accomplice was snatching his duffle bag!

Lenny bolted aimlessly in the direction that the woman rushed off in, and was barely able to pick up the scent of her pungent perfume, until he stumbled on a secluded narrow staircase.

He continued to follow the smell down the staircase into a remote hallway where the scent continued to grow stronger and stronger until it ended outside of a private employee restroom.

Lenny cautiously turned the doorknob, but it was locked.

He reached behind his back and removed Big Al's large chrome gun and tapped the butt of it on the restroom door.

"Occupied!" shouted the deep voice of an annoyed man from within.

Lenny continued tapping on the door until he heard the latch aggressively unlock, and the door briskly swung open!

Standing there was a very large and angry black man, wearing a purple fur pimp hat, which matched his purple suit and purple patent leather shoes!

He was aggressively postured there, and was surprised to see that Lenny had found him.

"Get lost corn bread, or I'll waste your honkey ass!" the pimp angrily shouted, and then he raised the Tommy gun which he had discovered in Lenny's duffle bag, and pointed it at his head!

"That ain't gonna work without the bullet drum, slick!" Lenny calmly stated, and then he raised and pointed his fancy chrome pistol at the man's head and instantly pulled the trigger!

He quickly grabbed the machine gun away from him before the man's body hit the floor, and he continued stepping over him as he quickly entered the restroom.

Inside, in a doorless toilet stall was the prostitute cowering on top of the toilet, and his duffle bag was just sitting there wide open on the sink.

"Please don't kill me! He made me do it!" she cried.

Lenny placed the machine gun back into his duffle bag, and quickly inspected that all its contents were still intact.

He glanced over at the girl and then grabbed her by her hair and dragged her out of the stall!

She screamed and kicked at him until he pointed his pistol at her face.

"Shut up and do what I tell ya, and you just might walk out of here alive!" Lenny shouted.

She instantly quieted down and became submissive trying to compose herself as she glanced over at her pimps' lifeless body, and his brains splattered all over the bathroom wall.

Lenny ordered her to take off her clothes and to get down on her knees. She readily complied, realizing that this might just be her last chance to save herself, and she was prepared to do whatever she had to do.

"We're going to play a little game called "Milk the Cow," Lenny snickered.

"Anything you want baby," she nervously replied.

As Lenny began unzipping his pants, he suddenly heard the loud blast of a train whistle blowing, and he quickly glanced at his stolen watch.

It was 12:35!

"Shit! I'm gonna miss my train!" he shouted.

He quickly gathered up his duffle bag and her clothes!

He ordered the woman to stay put, and not to come out of the bathroom or his "friend" who was waiting outside would gun her down.

He ran out of the restroom as fast as he could, and tossed her clothes onto the tracks as he raced to gate 23!

The train was just beginning to leave the station as Lenny finally arrived at the gate.

He ran as fast as he could, while stumbling along with the large duffle bag in tow.

With no second chances, he leapt onto the loading platform and barely made it onto the train!

He stumbled through the door while trying to catch his breath, and discovered that the train was mostly empty, and so he quickly found a seat and settled in for the long ride to Chicago.

As he sat there, his heart was still pounding, and he could still smell the sweet fragrance of that hookers cheap perfume.

He was proud of himself that he was able to reclaim his goods!

He felt that he accomplished a lot that night, and thought about how his luck had finally changed, and now he wasn't that loser anymore that his father always said he was.

Chapter 12

The train ride was very long and arduous, and made numerous stops throughout the night.

Lenny was unpleasantly surprised when the train actually stopped in Binghamton, his home town.

He thought for a moment how freaked out his family would be if he just showed up on their doorstep.

"Maybe I could sneak back to the farm and kill them all while they were sleeping," he manically thought.

He began reflecting about his mother and father, and how they turned their backs on him when he was down and out in reform school.

And how Georgie beat him to a pulp that night, causing him to run away from home with no money, which coerced him into robbing the gas station attendant.

And then there was Sonny boy.

Lenny hated his whole family, but he despised Sonny the most.

"If it wasn't for Sonny being born, things would have been a lot different for me. I would have been the golden child, and I would have been showered with all their love and attention!

Someday I will go back to the farm, and show them what happens to people who cross me! I'll show them all one day!" scorned Lenny.

It wasn't until about 3 PM that the train had finally arrived in Chicago.

By then the train was full of commuters, and it was easy for Lenny to just blend in with the crowd as the train emptied and the passengers poured out into the busy streets of Chicago.

He moved along with the swarm of people into the street, and from there he decided to explore the city, and see what opportunities might pass his way.

The city life was new to him, considering that he was just a farm boy from Binghamton, New York.

He took a deep breath and suddenly realized why they called Chicago the "Windy City."

The gusts of wind coming off the lake were strong, and he didn't have anything else to wear other than the blood spattered clothes on his back.

He continued on until he stumbled on a men's clothing store, and decided he had earned himself a suave new gangster outfit.

He had traded in his worn out jeans and blood stained flannel shirt for a dark gray pinstripe suit, and a white cotton cufflinked shirt with a wide black and white striped tie.

His sneakers were tossed for a new pair of black and white patent leather wing tipped shoes. And to top it all off, a dark gray fedora hat with a wide black band and a blue bird feather.

These clothes made him feel like a new and powerful man, and he actually looked quite fashionable and he definitely fit the gangster image.

He had never had new clothes or shoes before, and always got stuck with Georgies "Hand me downs."

When he left the shop toting his duffle bag, he noticed a photography studio which had a large flashing light bulb sign above the window.

"Neumann's Photography Studio... Photographer of the Rich and Famous" and so he decided to have his picture taken.

He cautiously walked inside and was immediately surrounded by hundreds of black and white images hanging on the walls. Some pictures were of very famous people, but there were others that made him sick to his stomach. Family pictures of affluent parents with their silver spooned children. Pictures of mother's holding and kissing their babies, and fathers playing ball with their sons.

Lenny began to get angry at the fact that he never had any fond memories of his childhood, just pain and anguish. His blood began to boil and then he immediately began ripping the pictures off the wall and then he turned around and angrily kicked the door open and strutted out.

Chapter 13

The streets of Chicago were alive and busy with hundreds of thousands of people living their lives there.

However, Chicago in the late 1950's was far from safe, and it was filled with thugs, thieves and gangsters.

The cops who were there to serve and protect, for the most part were often more crooked than the gangsters themselves.

Lenny was looking to join up with the mob, and he thought Chicago might just be the right place for him.

After just arriving, he wandered throughout the city, and as the balance of the day wore on, he became tired and sat down on a park bench near the lake, and dozed off for a bit.

A short time later, the sun was setting and he was rudely awakened by a policeman.

"Move it boy, before I run you in for vagrancy!" commanded the stern officer, and he raised his nightstick at Lenny.

Lenny instinctively reached behind his back where his pistol was concealed and pulled the hammer back.

Suddenly, in the distance a woman screamed, and it turned the officer's attention away from Lenny.

"Now beat it!" the police officer shouted at Lenny, and then he bolted toward the direction of the woman's scream.

Lenny got up and continued on, aimlessly walking the streets of Chicago. However, now he was absorbed by a new empowerment that he never felt before.

Lenny with a loaded gun was a dangerous affair for anyone he came across. He had tasted blood and was anxious to kill again. It didn't matter if it was a police officer or even a child, he was out of control and looking to feed his appetite for murder.

Lenny spent the rest of the night wandering throughout the streets of the city just looking for something to happen.

At one point he stumbled into the red light district, and was approached by several prostitutes who were trying to entice him into a good time.

The fear of being ripped off again by hookers, kept him from caving in, and he ignored them, and just kept on walking.

It was about 10 PM when he turned a corner and noticed the brightly lit white and blue neon marquise sign of the Chicago Hotel, and decided it was about time to find a place to stay for the night.

As he headed toward the hotel's entrance, he was suddenly startled as he heard several loud gunshots ringing out from behind him!

When he turned, he noticed a long black Cadillac speeding away from the scene, and its tires screeched at every turn!

A thin middle aged man was lying on the street riddled with bullet holes, coughing up blood and struggling to breath.

Lenny raced over to him to see what had happened, and he noticed a black satchel that was hidden underneath the dying man's trench coat.

The man believing Lenny to be a good Samaritan begged Lenny for help! But instead, Lenny wrestled the satchel away from the dying man, and kicked him several times in the head before running off with his bag!

Inside that bag, Lenny discovered a trove of betting receipts which included the betters' names and the money they owed.

There was also a few hundred dollars in an envelope, a pair of brass knuckles, a small black wooden billy club filled with lead and several business cards from a pizza restaurant called "Sedone's of Chicago" inside the satchel.

"Wait a minute, that's gotta be Big Al's brother's place!" thought Lenny.

He remembered seeing that restaurant in the photograph he found inside Big Al's safe and it was actually in his duffle bag.

"Hmmm, this could be really interesting. I'm feeling a little hungry for a pizza tonight," Lenny chuckled to himself.

Chapter 14

Lenny was now determined and on a mission.

With his duffle bag and newfound satchel in tow, he decided to make his way over to the "Sedone's of Chicago" pizza parlor.

Ironically he had to ask another police officer for directions, and by the time he finally found it, it was close to midnight, and it seemed that the restaurant was closed.

He proceeded down a side alley, and then around the back of the restaurant where he found the rear door of the restaurant to be slightly ajar, and he overheard voices. Loud voices coming from the restaurant's kitchen area.

As he gently nudged the door open a bit more with his foot, he could hear a group of people crying hysterically, as if they were going to be killed.

He also overheard an Italian man's deep voice in a panicked state, begging for their lives.

"Please don't kill us!! You can have all of Chicago! In the safe, I have $25,000 dollars! It's yours, take it and go!" the man cried.

"Tough luck, Sedone. Mr. G don't like you cutting in on his action, and we already took out most of your boys tonight.

You and your gang are finished, but thanks for telling me about the 25 grand in your safe! Would you mind handing it over so we don't have to drag the whole tin can back to Mr. G's garage!" snickered the gunman.

It was an extremely undignified scene for Lenny to watch.

Everyone was hysterically screaming and crying, and begging for their lives.

"What a bunch of doormats," Lenny thought.

Lenny then cautiously peeked into the doorway, and observed eight thugs with machine guns, aiming their weapons at several men and a woman who were lined up facing a wall, and they were all blubbering away.

He spotted Sedone who was a large older Italian man, who had a strong family resemblance to Big Al.

There was also a very pretty woman, with several other heavy-set mobster looking men, and oddly a black man who also seemed to be part of the gang.

Lenny lackadaisically reached into his duffle bag, and removed the Tommy gun, and snapped on a full drum of ammunition.

He pulled back the chambering bolt on the gun and calmly made his entrance.

"Hey, is this a bad time to order a pizza?!" Lenny called out.

Then he squeezed the trigger on his gun, and opened fire on the eight armed thugs.

Loud repetitive gunfire, ricocheting bullets and smoke filled the room, as Lenny emptied his machine gun.

He annihilated the gang in a matter of seconds, and their contorted bodies fell to the floor like acorns falling off an oak tree…dead.

Not realizing what was happening, Sedone and his gang also collapsed to the floor believing it was them who was being fired upon as well.

When the smoke began to clear, Sedone nervously looked over his shoulder and noticed Lenny standing there at the back door still clutching his smoldering machine gun.

It was then that Sedone jubilantly realized that his enemy was now in fact dead, and they were still very much alive!

"Minga! You are my angel!" rejoiced Sedone!

"My boy, I am going to make you a rich and famous man for what you have done for us tonight!"

Lenny handed over the satchel, and told Sedone that he recovered it from a dying man who had asked him to return it to his boss.

"Thank you my boy, that was my book collector, Salvator," stated Sedone.

"I tried to help him by holding him and reciting a prayer for the lug as he was dying," Lenny mournfully stated (Flashback to the scene, Lenny kicking the man abusively as he steals the satchel).

"Ya know Pop...not for nothin' but whoever sent these goons out to put the hit on you, thinks you're all dead by now. Maybe you should send your boys out and give it back to 'em!" exclaimed Lenny.

Sedone snapped his fingers and ordered his men to get their guns, and head down to "The Green Mill Cafe" where he knew Bobby G and his gang would be celebrating Sedones demise.

"Make sure you bring me that son a ma bitch Bobby G's finger! With the ring on it! And take these dead bastards with you!

After you finish Bobby G, take them for a boat ride and dump them in the lake!" shouted Sedone.

In an instant, the men gathered their guns and ran out toting all sorts of artillery while dragging dead bodies away with them.

"You boy stay here, what's your name boy?" kindly questioned Sedone.

"My name is Lenny."

"Are you an Italian or Sicilian?" questioned Sedone.

"Neither, I'm a badass German flunky from Binghamton, New York," proudly replied Lenny.

"I am Sedone, and from now on you work for me, kid. All the free pizza you can eat, and I promise to make you a rich and respected man if you agree!

This is my girlfriend Ava, she's my wife's cousin but don't tell my wife if you know what I mean, kiddo!" chuckled Sedone.

Ava rushed over to Lenny and hugged and kissed him in gratitude for saving her life. He cringed, since he was not accustomed to women fawning all over him.

"You are a big man kid, on account you gave those lousy punks the real business, come let's eat pizza!" exclaimed Sedone.

Lenny did feel like a big man now, since this was the first time ANYONE has ever told him he did something good.

As far as being Big…Lenny was maybe 170 pounds dripping wet.

My brother Georgie and I inherited my dad's John Wayne physique, where Lenny was the runt of the litter compared to us.

But now he considered himself a big man and it fed his ego, and his need to prove to our father that he wasn't a "good for nothing" after all.

Suddenly their celebration was interrupted by the phone ringing.

It was a long distance call for Sedone.

His cousin Rocko from New York City was calling with tragic news.

"No, no, it can't be true!!" shouted Sedone.

He recklessly hung up the phone and collapsed onto a chair, and with grave despair he began to cry hysterically all over again.

"Someone killed my brother Alberto last night, in New York City!!" he shouted in vain.

"I'm so sorry, how did it happen?" Lenny solemnly questioned.

"I'm told some assassin beat him to death with a steel pipe in his restaurant! That's all I know! His step son Joey and most of his gang were also killed!" cried Sedone.

"Where are the stinkin' cops when you need them?" remarked Lenny.

"I won't rest until I get the bastard that did this to my brother!" shouted Sedone. "NEVER!!!"

Chapter 15

As the years passed by, we never heard from or spoke of Lenny, and eventually it just became easier to just forget about him.

Occasionally someone would ask if we ever heard from him, but my father would just shrug his shoulders and say that Lenny was gone, and hopefully not getting into trouble. Little did we know that he was actually linked up with the Chicago mob and he became a cold blooded killer.

My parents were getting on in years, and Georgie, who finally did manage to scrape up enough money to attend college in New York City, left the farm and received a degree in electronics.

We all thought that he would ultimately return to the area, and maybe start a business while helping out at the farm. Considering that he would someday inherit the farm, there was a lot riding on his return.

But to no avail, and with intense pressure from my father for him to return, he decided that he preferred city life to milking cows and baling hay.

He told my father that he could make 100 times more money than my father made by selling and repairing electronic equipment, and without the daily grudge of having to tend to animals and hard labor everyday.

"Sonny will take care of the farm, he is more like you, Dad" he told my father.

My parents were very disappointed but understood that farm life and country living wasn't for everyone, especially after Georgie had a taste of living in the city.

Although Georgie sometimes came for visits, it was obvious he was uncomfortable on the farm and seldom stayed for more than a day or two.

Life in the country was too slow and boring for him compared to living in the big city. Pretty girls, fancy restaurants and making lots of money were too much for him to resist.

I was now eighteen and out of guilt, made the commitment to stay and help my father on the farm, but I secretly wished that I could be with Georgie in the big city.

I just couldn't leave the farm and my elderly parents with no help, and so I stayed.

I attended a local college and managed to meet a lot of pretty girls there, but there was always something missing, and things never worked out. I guess once they realized they would be stuck on the farm too, I wasn't very appealing.

It wasn't easy living at home, going to college and working on the farm.

Most of the farm work was on me now. We couldn't afford to hire anymore psychopaths, and so many bad memories because of Lenny, especially those poor little sparrows.

The twine and their tiny skeletal remains were still tangled up in our sycamore tree.

Sometimes I would run into Lenny's old friend, Eugene though.

He tries to avoid me now, since I outgrew the bastard. But I never forgot about my brother's accomplice, and how terribly they both treated me.

I suppose he's afraid I might be harboring some sort of a grudge, and maybe come to remember how he and Lenny tormented me. Maybe I might just take some sweet revenge out on him. He certainly had it coming, if I did.

But one day I ran into Eugene at the hardware store. He got really nervous and uncomfortable when he saw me, but he finally got up the nerve and approached me.

"I suppose I owe you an apology, Sonny. You know there weren't a lot of kids my age in our neck of the woods, in the desolate area where we lived.

It seemed that Lenny was the only friend option that I had at the time.

In the beginning it was fun hanging out with him on your farm. There was always something fun to do. But, as time went on, Lenny started to become more and more aggressive, violent and psychotic.

That's when I started to fear him, and I felt trapped. If I rocked his boat or told him I was done being friends with him, he would have turned on me, and everyone knew how Lenny handled things.

For the most part, I just went along with him, and I didn't know how to break free of him without the blowback. I suffered for it too. I was an outcast at school because people knew we were friends, and nobody wanted to be friends with me if I was Lenny's friend.

"Guilt by Association" a girl I once asked out replied to me.

That night after the basketball game, when Lenny got jumped on our way to the parking lot, you pleaded with me to help him. Hell, I seriously hoped and prayed that those guys were going to kill him, so then I could finally be free of Lenny's grip!

I just want to tell you that I'm sorry, Sonny." Eugene solemnly stated, and he reached out to shake my hand.

I actually understood what he meant, but I still felt that he took a lot of pleasure out of antagonizing me, along with Lenny.

I certainly could never trust Eugene, and I wasn't ever going to be friends with him, but there was no sense in fostering a festering grudge.

And so I ceremoniously shook his hand, but with it I gave him a long hard squeeze, just so that he understood that I wouldn't forget the horrible things they put me through, and that now I could indisputably kick his ass, if and when, I ever felt like it.

Sadly, a few months later he was drafted to serve in the Vietnam war, and was never the same after he came home.

His unit was in charge of clearing helicopter landing areas in the jungle.

While they were working behind enemy lines they were ambushed, and everyone was killed except for Eugene. His arm was severely lacerated, but he healed himself by licking his wounds, just as an animal would do.

He was imprisoned in a remote hell hole of a POW encampment deep in a desolate area of the jungle, where they kept him in a banana crate hung high over a huge fire pit by a thin frayed hemp rope.

Sometimes his captors would bring him down and let him out of the crate, but it was either to do grunge work around the camp or more often to be made as an object of their hideous amusement.

He was worked and tortured to near death for two years before he was finally liberated by a group of Green Berets.

When they rescued him, Eugene's sunken face was covered by his long lice infested beard, and he was emaciated. He was only surviving off eating insects and the occasional rat that he could catch, and grotesquely tear apart and eat raw.

When he was rescued, he was only wearing a filthy tattered loincloth, and his skin was severely mangey, riddled with scabs, and ravaged by lice and large jungle mosquitoes. He had dozens of gruesome scars, and bloody contusions all over his body from the abuse he received by the hands of his captors.

The group of soldiers who rescued him were so angered and disgusted by what they saw, that they lined up all the prison guards in front of the fire pit, and the squad Captain handed Eugene an M60 machine gun, loaded with a full bandolier of bullets.

The Captain placed his hand on Eugene's shoulder and ordered him to guard the prisons as they searched for more survivors, and with that he gave him the nod of retribution.

The prison guards instantly began to scream and shout wildly, despite the fact that none of them understood English!

However, they were all well aware of what was happening.

Arming Eugene and then putting him in charge of overseeing them was their death sentence!

Minutes after the Green Berets disbursed and left him alone, he recounted the two years of horrific torture these animals had bestowed upon him.

Deadly games of Russian roulette, hanging him by his arms by a piece of wire for days at a time and urinating all over him, and forcing him to dig out their latrine with his bare hands are just a few of the sickening deeds these tormentors bestowed upon him.

None of them ever showed him an inkling of kindness or compassion.

He gritted his teeth and then he pulled the trigger back on his machine gun, and began relentlessly gunning them all down!

Killing them all over and over again, until his gun was finally empty!

He was later admitted to a military psychiatric hospital, and stayed there for about a year before they kicked him out on the street.

They said he wasn't a danger to society and he just needed a little more time to be back with his family.

Truth is, his family was scared shitless of him, and didn't want him back either. No one knew what was going on inside Eugene's head because he refused to talk to anyone.

Everyone considered him to be a ticking time bomb, except the VA hospital. With no other options his parents reluctantly took him in.

Eugene lives with his parents now, and just stays at home.

His head is not right, and he still doesn't talk to anyone.

Rain or shine, he just sits on their porch all day on an old western wagon wheel rocking chair, rocking back and forth and staring out at the world he left behind. Searching out there for something, but sadly no one really knows for sure what it is. Maybe he is waiting for the Green Berets to rescue him again, to take away those horrific memories of the war.

Chapter 16

Tragically, it was one of those days where nothing seemed to go right. I woke up with a nervous ache in my stomach, but couldn't understand why.

The eastern dawn sky was bright red and I remembered the old sailors credo stating; "Red sky at night, sailors delight. Red sky in the morning, sailors warning." and I knew that the morning red sky meant a storm was brewing. Other than that, I had no reason to be feeling as if something dreadful was going to happen, but it loomed over me.

Later that morning my mother and I ventured off to the feed co-op to pick up an order of goods for the farm, when my father frantically telephoned the store looking for us.

He was suddenly having a lot of difficulty breathing caused by his emphysema, which he acquired several years ago due to his chain smoking of those filterless Lucky Strike cigarettes for most of his life.

His health had been gradually deteriorating over the years, but he refused to ever go to see a doctor for help, stating that;

"They were all a bunch of crooks."

The store manager appeared to be very concerned and handed me the phone.

My dad was nervously upset and he began yelling at me.

"What the hell is taking you so long?! I can't breathe and I think I need to go to the hospital!" he shouted.

After all these years of wheezing and difficulty breathing, now he decides he wants to go see a doctor? Something must be terribly wrong.

"Get your damn asses...in the truck...and come home now!" he wheezed.

Then he abruptly hung up on me.

My mom was worried, and suggested that she would get a ride back to the farm with a neighbor who was just leaving the feed store, and that I should just stay and finish loading the supplies. Reluctantly I agreed.

Shortly thereafter, when I returned to the farm, there was a police car and an ambulance parked in our driveway.

I jumped out of the truck praying to God that my dad was still alive, and all this commotion was just all about an ambulance ride to the hospital, where he would be treated with oxygen and then sent back home.

That nervous "sick to my stomach" feeling that I had when I woke up was now more apparent, and my knees became weak as I raced toward the house. The front door was wide open, and I found my mother sitting and crying at the kitchen table with a police officer trying to console her.

The paramedics were rolling a gurney past me with a large body covered with a white sheet from head to toe, and my heart sunk.

When she saw me, my mother jumped up and embraced me.

She sobbed uncontrollably, and I knew that meant my father was gone.

All I could think of was what the last thing my father had said to me;

"Get your damn asses in the truck, and come home now!" and he abruptly hung up the phone without even saying goodbye to me.

Unfortunately, it wasn't the "I'm so proud of you son, or I love you, Sonny." That would have given me some comfort, knowing that at least he had something nice to say to me before he died.

I stayed up with my mom all night, and there was an eerie emptiness in the house without my father.

After the funeral, Georgie told me to take care of mom, and he got in his car and drove off.

We never heard from Lenny, not really expecting to see him at the funeral.

We didn't even know how to contact him, not that we would have even if we did know where he was.

That door was best left closed.

As the months carried on, I continued to run the farm as usual for my mom, but in the beginning it was difficult not having my father around.

It was terrible losing my father, but as hard as it was, I felt grateful that I still had my mom. I was once told;

"You are not a man until you lose your father"

I didn't get it until now.

I felt as if I had the weight of the world on my shoulders, and I didn't have my father to lean on, to ask for his advice or guidance anymore.

Now I had to fill his shoes, and take care of the farm and my mother.

I was fortunate to have a man like my father in my life.

For whatever I had gratefully learned from my father, will forever be within me.

Now I am a man.

Chapter 17

It was a difficult time after my father had passed.

My mother was very depressed, and she was moping around wishing that it was her, rather than my father who died.

Georgie occasionally called, but rarely visited.

He chose to stay away leaving me to take care of our mother and the farm. He was fortunate, he didn't have to deal with her or it.

Thankfully, over time she got better, and she actually had discovered her new found freedom. She could do whatever she wanted without my fathers permission.

Georgie had actually moved out of New York City, and he opened a new business in Brookfield, Illinois. He had a girlfriend that he met in college from that area, and he wanted to be closer to her. Her father offered to help him monetarily to set up his business, but unfortunately, all that fell through several months after he had moved out there.

Unfortunately, Georgie caught his girlfriend cheating on him, when she had a one night stand with an old boyfriend.

He actually caught them in the act when he just happened to show up at her apartment early one morning. He broke things up a bit, then he broke things off with her, even though she begged him to give her a second chance.

But Georgie was hurt and he replied to her;

"Once a cheater, always a cheater!" and he walked out the door for good.

With everything still in place, he continued on with his venture, and opened his electronics store that he named "Georgie's TV and Radio Barn." He frequently told his vendors that he grew up on a farm, and now instead of milking cows he's milking his customers.

When he informed my mother that he was moving to Illinois and opening up a new business, she was afraid that he was going to fail.

"Who's going to buy those expensive electronical things? You'll lose your shirt!" she criticized.

He replied;

"Televisions are the new rage and everyone will be able to afford one, and they are the business of the future, and besides I have another shirt in my closet!"

Personally, I prefer being outside in the fresh air, and not dealing with the busy customer shuffle. It was a big risk, and not having much money to start with was going to be difficult for him.

The down side was, Georgie was constantly asking me and my mother if we would loan him money for his business. My mom didn't have much, but he knew she couldn't say no to him, and he was constantly pressing her for more money.

He took whatever she could send him. I had some money saved, but I needed it for my future, and because I wasn't as soft as my mother, it was easier for me to say no to him.

As a way to entice me, he was constantly asking me to come work for him. He said if I came to work for him, he would make me a manager, and pay me minimum wage under the table.

He was trying to convince me that it was like getting paid twice as much since the taxes would not be taken out.

I responded that it was still poverty level wages and I would get a refund of the taxes withheld anyways… "Gee thanks, Georgie!"

Besides, who was going to help my mom on the farm? He knew I could never leave her.

When I finally caved in and did actually loan him some money, he never paid me back, and I rarely heard from him again. It got awkward whenever he called, and I answered the phone. Sometimes he would just quickly hang up right away, and other times he would just say "Let me talk to mom."

Shortly thereafter he totally stopped coming to visit, and he rarely called at all after that.

My father used to say;

"Never loan money to someone you like. Because you will never see them again."

I always felt that the opposite of that statement could be more beneficial;

"Only loan money to someone you don't like. And if you are fortunate, you will never see them again!"

Since he never made any effort to pay me back, I didn't believe that his store was doing that well, despite what he was telling everyone.

Although we were once very close, it wasn't the same between Georgie and me anymore.

He changed as the years went on, and he became more obsessed with taking care of Georgie, rather than worrying about me and our mother at the farm.

Maybe someday we can be close again. If he ever pays me back.

Chapter 18

A year has passed since my father's death, and my mother and I are bonded closer than ever. She began depending on me to be the man of the house just as if I were my father.

She tells everyone she would be lost without me, and that puts a lot of pressure on me to stick around and keep working the farm.

It's been very difficult without my father around.

My mother was totally dependent on him, although there was a balance between them.

He took care of the farm and she was in charge of the house.

I didn't realize until now what a financial undertaking the farm was.

I don't think she did either.

They were barely making a living from the farm before my father died, yet my parents always seemed to find a way to make sure we always had what we needed.

Now that he is gone, it's becoming a real challenge to make enough money on our farm goods, especially since trucking has expanded and supermarkets are now able to purchase their products cheaper from monster dairy farms, who are equipped to milk over 500 cows at a time. We only have about eighty five cows.

Hopefully, I can keep the farm going for my mother's sake, but I'm afraid we can't go on much longer this way.

Then one hot humid summer evening as my mother and I sat at the kitchen table playing cards after supper, there was a knock at our front screen door.

As I hastily arose from the table to see who was there, I was mentally preparing excuses to get rid of the pest who I presumed was going to be standing there at our front door…That relentless Fuller Brush salesman.

He always appeared at the most awkward times in hopes of catching us off guard, and pitching us with his latest cleaning products and brushes.

"We don't need any more toilet brushes or butt cream!" I shouted as I drudged over to the door.

However, I was shocked when I pushed the screen door open, only to find that there was no Fuller Brush man there, but a beautiful young woman.

"Mr. Kuhr, I'm definitely not here to sell you Butt cream!" she joked.

I was so embarrassed! A wave of heated perspiration wrapped itself around me like a steaming face towel at a barber shop!

"I actually thought you were that pesky Fuller Brush guy," I awkwardly chuckled.

"I know who you are talking about. That guy is ridiculously aggressive. He once stuck his foot in the door at my parents house, and wouldn't leave until my mom bought some brass cleaner. The funny thing was, we didn't even have anything made of brass in the house!" she laughed.

"By the way my name is Lass," and she handed me her business card.

I took her card and was disappointed to see that she was another real estate agent from a land development company sniffing around to buy our farm.

"Hi, I'm Sonny, and you're beautiful but we're not selling," I replied.

She smiled and blushed at the compliment, and went on to say that she was representing someone who was interested in buying our farm.

This was not the first time anyone had reached out to my parents to buy the place.

Now that my father was gone, there were so many emotional ties to the farm for my mother, and now as my father had always done, she continued on with the family tradition of chasing real estate agents off our property.

The sentimental feelings my mother was holding onto was her way to hang on to the things she loved most, and the memories of her husband.

She lost Lenny to crime, Georgie to the city and her husband to smoking.

The farm had kept her close to me, and she was afraid that without the farm, I would leave her too.

Unfortunately, my mother had a jealous streak and she made it difficult for me to date women.

I think she dreaded that I might fall in love with someone who would take me away from her, and she would be alone.

No one was ever good enough for her Sonny boy, and she always found something wrong with the girls I dated, and hated them.

When my mother heard me talking to a young lady at the door, she drifted right over to investigate.

"Mom, this pretty girl has someone who wants to buy the farm. How much do you want for it? Or should I just get the shotgun and run her off the property?" I joked.

I was expecting her to tell "Lass" to get "Losst."

But instead, she immediately softened, and she invited the young woman in.

We all sat down at the kitchen table, and the young woman introduced herself to my mother and shook her hand.

"Hey, how come I didn't get a handshake!" I protested.

"I would have Sonny, but then I was afraid you might have butt cream all over your fingers!" she joked.

My mother awkwardly laughed as she didn't know what Lass was talking about, but her quick wit was very impressive.

"That was so funny, you should be on The Ed Sullivan show!" I chuckled.

But she was so stunningly beautiful, I couldn't take my eyes off of her.

If she would have said "The sky was chicken liver brown," I would have laughed at that too.

As we sat there listening to her pitch, it was extremely difficult for me to concentrate on what she was saying.

Her perfume was captivating, and all I could think of was;

"Where has this gift from God been hiding all my life!"

Her hazel brown eyes, her dark mahogany hair that subtly draped her face, and her smile that lit up the room. She was gorgeous!

I wasn't paying attention, but out of the corner of her eye, my mother was observing me as I was becoming enchanted by Lass, and when she made a loud "Ahemm" sound as if her throat was clogged with my obvious infatuation, it snapped me back into reality.

I had no chance with this girl. She was way out of my league. I was just a poor farm boy and she was a rich and fancy city girl.

Lass continued, and went on to say that she just started working for her father, and this was the first time she had ever "knocked" on anyone's door, soliciting business for him.

We all knew her father very well, since he was a big time land developer in the area.

He had been to our house many times before, always inquiring if my father would sell him the farm.

But, my father had no patience for the man, and he would throw him off the property each and every time he showed up.

Once my father was so aggravated with the man, that he actually pulled a shotgun on him, and he hightailed it off the farm and never returned!

I pray he never told Lass about that.

He was persistent, though not as persistent as the Fuller Brush man!

She went on to inform us that she had just graduated and moved back from college because she needed to help her father.

Her mother had recently passed away several months ago from a heart attack and her father was having a hard time coping with her loss, and she began to tear up. She was having a hard time with it, too.

I could see that she had a soft heart, and my mother seemed to like her... a lot.

"You know Missy, my handsome boy Sonny is single, are you dating anyone?" my mother inquired.

I almost fell out of the wobbly kitchen chair that I was sitting on when she blurted that out!

It was so embarrassing! Even more so than the butt cream incident! I wanted to crawl under the table and kill myself!!

"Sorry about that, I need to apologize for my mother…she has gone off the wagon and has been drinking moonshine all day!" I choked out, as I stared cold heartedly at my mother.

"Oh Sonny, now that was funny! And on that note I have to go.

I know you don't want to sell your beautiful farm, but if you ever change your mind, it would get my father off my back! Oh and by the way, no I don't have a boyfriend," she cheerfully stated and winked at me.

She then stood up and hugged my mother goodbye.

I walked with her to her car which was parked in our driveway, near the old sycamore tree which hung over our front porch.

She looked up into the tree and asked me why there was twine entangled up high in the tree branches.

The twine Lenny had used tying those poor sparrows together was still visible.

I told her it was from a kite that had gotten stuck up there when I was a boy.

I couldn't tell her what really happened, so I quickly changed the subject and I asked her about her name.

"That's an interesting name you have, Lass. Is that a nickname or a shortened name?" I questioned.

It was obvious that it made Lass become a bit uncomfortable with that question, but she replied that it was a shortened version of her full name.

"So do I have to guess or are you going to tell me what your name is?" I persisted.

"Actually, I would prefer you to guess, because I'm a little shy to tell you," she softly replied.

"Is it Lassie?" I joked.

"Nooo, good guess though! But I do love that dog!" she laughed.

I was stumped and was drawing a complete blank until it hit me.

"Oh my gosh is it Lass-t Chance?" I blurted out.

"Nope, but this is your last chance, and then I have to go," she remarked.

"It couldn't possibly be a silly name like Las Vegas, okay I give up," I said.

When Lass heard me say that, she froze and her face turned beet red.

"Your parents named you Las Vegas?!" I teased, and it seemed to rustle her feathers.

"Listen Sonny sky's, my parents met in Las Vegas and were married there too! It was a special place for them, and they thought it was romantic to name their only adorable child after a place that was so significant to their wonderful relationship! Besides who names their kid, Sunny!

Are you from some Aztec tribe or something!" jeered Lass.

It was obviously a sore spot for her, since she was most likely ribbed about it since grammar school.

She then stormed off to her car and fumbled with her keys.

I was left standing there, and I sensed my ship was sinking if it wasn't already sunk.

I raced over and stopped her from opening her car door, and she hastily turned to me.

"I'm so sorry, I really didn't want to hurt your feelings! My parents named me Sonikphart, after my great great German grandfather. Supposedly in Germany that's a pretty important name, but over here not so much. How do you think I felt when the kids at school were shouting that one out!"

Lass burst out laughing, and we both agreed that my name was worse.

My adrenaline switch had just flipped on, and it was time to either do or die for this farm boy.

I wanted to ask her to go on a date with me, but after what had just happened, and the fact that she was so out of my league, I felt she would most likely decline, and my heart would be crushed forever.

On the other hand, my father always used to say;

"Sonikphart, you can't hit a home run unless you stand up to bat."

I remembered his words of wisdom and it gave me courage to face this woman.

"Okay, batter up, Sonikphart!" I thought to myself.

I could feel my blood pressure rising as sweat began to permeate through my pores and drench my body. It was so damn humid or was it just me?

My heart was pounding like a bass drum as I looked into her beautiful hazel eyes.

I was working up the nerve to ask this angel who dropped from heaven, to go on a date with me.

"Umm uhh, Lass...Vegas"

I strained and struggled to get my words in order.

She just stood there leaning against her car while patiently looking at her fingernails and watching me struggle to speak, and she seemed to be enjoying herself as she was observing me crash and burn.

But then out of nowhere, she suddenly reached up with her two soft slender hands, and grabbed me by my sweat soaked work shirt, and pulled me close into her warm body and seductively whispered,

"Pick me up tomorrow night at 7 Sonny," then she kissed me on the lips, and then shoved me away from herself, and then she quickly hopped into her pearl white Thunderbird and started the engine, and sped out of our driveway.

I was left standing there in disbelief, and in a state of jubilant shock.

As I drifted back into the house, my mother was standing by the door.

"You better not let her get away Sonny, she's a good one," stated my mother.

I thought that was extremely odd coming from the woman who hated all my previous girlfriends.

"Mom don't you get it...they want to buy our farm...why else would she want to go out with me?" I replied.

"Sonny, strong handsome men like you are hard to come by, don't sell yourself short," she gloated.

"We'll see Ma… But I thought you hate all the women that I date?" I questioned.

"I usually do, but not this one Sonny, she's not like the usual losers you go out with!" she chuckled.

I just shook my head in disbelief and we sat back down and continued playing cards.

Chapter 19

I was extremely nervous, and had a queasy feeling all day long waiting for 7 o'clock to arrive, for my date with Lass.

I felt as if a big loaf like me had no chance with a girl like her.

Obviously she was only being nice to me to soften us up, so we would sell them the farm.

After the sale, she'll cool it off and ditch me.

I was so convinced that she was only using me, that I was contemplating calling off the date.

It was almost 6:30 and I was putting on a clean pair of blue jeans and one of my Sunday dress up shirts, and although I was apprehensive, I was determined to push through my inhibitions and was excited and ready to go.

"What are you going to do with that Lassie girl tonight, Sonny?" my mother inquired.

"Her name is Lass Vegas, and since it's Thursday night, I was thinking about taking her to the horse auction," I replied.

"Oh no, no, no, Sonny! Not the horse auction, that's a terrible idea! She's a fancy city girl, she'll hate that smelly place! You should take her out and see a movie or maybe go out to eat at the Dairy Queen. City girls like that sort of thing you know," my mother suggested.

I nodded my head, and gave my mother a kiss on the cheek and walked outside to my truck.

I looked at the business card Lass handed me, and began to drive to her address which was printed on it.

I noticed a flower stand on the way, and thought it would be nice to bring her flowers, especially since I made such a mess about her name the day before and she got so upset with me about it.

She lived approximately 7 miles from my farm, and when I finally found her street, I expected to pull up to a big fancy mansion, and when I pulled into the driveway I was right, she actually did live in a big fancy mansion.

My nerves were getting the better of me as I prepared to get out of my truck and I marched onward up the brick walkway to my execution, only to be confronted by the big scary front door to her kingdom.

I felt so out of place standing there. I was just a local farm boy and she was a princess.

I was completely nerve wracked as I rang the doorbell, and it seemed to take forever as I stood there waiting for her to answer the door.

"Maybe she forgot about our date?" I thought.

Then I heard heavy footsteps coming toward the door, and I could vaguely see a bald headed man appearing through the frosted glass door panel.

Lass's father unlocked the door then aggressively swung the front door open, and he appeared quite unenthusiastic that I was there to pick up his daughter!

"Well, if it isn't the infamous Mr. Sonny Kuhr, that just showed up on my front doorstep! Why the last time I saw you, your father was chasing me off your porch with a shotgun!" exclaimed Lass's father.

"Uh, yes Sir, sorry about that. My father didn't especially like developers coming around. He thought that they were trying to "steal" our farm as he put it, Sir." I replied.

He squinted at me with his left eye, while looking me up and down with sheer disdain with the right eye. Then he sternly stared at me straight in my eyes for a moment, and then he aggressively reached out his hand to shake hands with me, while he metaphorically raised his leg and marked his territory at the same time.

It quickly turned into a sort of strong man hand wrestling competition, where we were both trying to squeeze and break each other's hand!

"Pretty good grip you got there, Sonny!" he strained.

"You too Sir, but I think you're breaking my hand!" I painfully replied, and then we both pulled our hands apart without releasing our grips.

It was an unspoken draw I suppose. But out of respect, I left him with his hand intact and his dignity. I could have easily squashed his puny grip like a baked potato in my hand, but where would that have gotten me? I was already in his dog house.

"So my daughter tells me you buy a lot of butt cream from the Fuller Brush guy? You got a problem with your anus or something, Sonny?" he jeered.

"No sir, we use massive amounts of butt cream on the milking cows teats," I replied.

"Teats?" inquired her father.

"Yes Sir, their teats. They get pretty abraded from the automatic milkers yanking on them, so I rub butt cream all over their teats," I awkwardly stated as I was demonstrating the milking action with my two hands.

Just then Lass came bouncing down the staircase wearing tight faded blue jeans, red cowboy boots, a black silk western shirt and a black cowboy hat. She looked so beautiful!

I handed her the flowers and she seemed to like them very much.

"Thank you Sonny, so what were you two boys talking about?" she inquired.

"Uhh, cow teats," I nervously blurted out.

She awkwardly turned to her father.

"Teats?" she ridiculously stated.

"Yep, teats," he smirked.

"Okay Sonny, we had better get going before you boys get started on castration and sperm collection!" Lass joked.

"Nice to see you again, Sir," I stated.

He didn't say anything back, he just growled and continued to give me his evil eyed stare as he watched us walk away toward my pickup truck.

"So I guess you passed my dad's test!" swooned Lass.

"It didn't seem to me like I passed anything!" I replied.

"Oh my father liked you a lot, otherwise he would have chased you off with his shotgun!" Lass chuckled.

"Funny, my father once chased him off our property with a shotgun, and he sure did remind me of it!" I exclaimed.

"I know Sonny, he made sure to tell me all about it when I told him you were taking me out tonight!" she laughed.

I opened the truck door for her and she hopped in.

And as I got in on the other side she slid all the way over next to me, almost sitting on top of me. She was smelling so good and looking so beautiful, but I was as nervous as a long tailed cat in a rocking chair factory.

I started the truck and I could see her father, still watching me from the front door.

He lifted his clenched hand and raised his thumb and pointer finger and made a gun with his two fingers and pointed it at me!

"So where are you taking me tonight, Sonny?" she exuberantly asked.

"Uhh, I was thinking about maybe going to the IHOP and then a movie?" I suggested.

She looked down at the floor and was disappointed.

"What's the matter Lass, don't you like pancakes for supper?" I dumbfoundly asked.

"Sonny, I thought you were going to be different from all the other boys who took me out," she sadly stated.

I shook my head in disbelief, and my mothers words were reverberating in my mind!

"Well, I really wanted to take you to the horse auction down in Kirkwood tonight, but my mom told me that it was a dumb idea because you were a fancy city girl, and so I went to plan B!" I exclaimed.

"Yahoo!! Let's go! That sounds like so much fun, Sonny! Are you gonna buy me a horse!" Lass shouted.

"Uhmm, uhh well, I didn't, well, uhmm," I stammered.

"I'm only kidding, Sonny. I just love watching you sweat!"

We drove for about an hour, and the conversation was entirely about horses.

When we finally arrived at the horse auction, we continued talking about our love of horses and her childhood as an equestrian horse jumper, and I told her about the fun times I had riding with Georgie on old Sarg.

The parking lot was packed with all sorts of sparkling new and old rust bucket horse trailers of all sizes, and hundreds of pick up trucks.

The horse auction was also the place to show off your fancy pickup truck. The more chrome, the bigger and fancier the rig and trailer combo, the more successful you appeared, even though they were all mostly in debt up to the hilt.

"It's a really busy night for horse trading," I commented.

Sellers were chaotically backing off horse's right off their trailers and prospective buyers were bronco riding them throughout the parking lot, taking them for test rides before they were run through the auction to avoid the hefty sales commissions and possibly strike a better deal.

It was always an interesting event, going to the horse auction because of the magnitude of crazy horse people there.

Sometimes you can find a good horse at the auction, but unfortunately this was the end of the road for many of the undesirable horses. Either they are just too old and no one wanted them anymore, or they had just come off the race track, injured or too slow to win.

Sometimes they were just problem horses with a possible medical condition such as chronic lameness issues, severe bodily injuries or they were deathly ill.

But there are also the "mental cases."

Those are the ones that habitually want to bite, kick, buck you off, flip over backward on top of you, or worst of all... no brakes included!

It's not a lot of fun being kidnapped on a runaway horse.

Galloping out of control as fast as that horse can run back to the barn! Or even more detrimental, running past the barn and out into the street with you, slipping and skidding through the oncoming traffic until you finally collide with a minivan!

Your life passes before you when you're on a runaway, and there is no kill switch!

You can contemplate jumping off, but there is a 50/50 chance that if you just hang on long enough, you might just survive.

Jumping off of an out of control horse could be far worse. It's a very hard landing, and your odds just shifted to 90/10 that you will be hurt pretty badly.

Whatever these horses' issues were, if they couldn't be sold from their backyards or farms, there was often a reason why they ended up at the horse auction.

So buyer beware! There won't be a pretty printed label attached to them either, stating;

"This horse has bowed tendons, navicular disease, congenital cough, can't chew hay because he doesn't have a tongue and will roll over on top of you while being ridden!"

You need to be an experienced horseman to know the signs of an injured or problematic horse.

Often though, there are horses with obvious catastrophic issues that no one wanted to buy.

For those unfortunate ones the horse meat agent or "The Grim Reaper" as many referred to him as, would scoop them up cheaply for slaughter.

It's a horrible ending for someone's longtime companion, or a faithful steed that just had the misfortune of just getting too old or injured.

Together we strolled through the massive barn which housed thousands of square metal holding pens. Each one contained several horses that were waiting for their turn to be auctioned off, or that had been returned just after being sold and were awaiting for the paperwork to clear before the buyer's were allowed to take them home.

There was a lot of commotion going on throughout the barn.

Horses were whinnying and calling for their former stablemates.

Some were kicking at each other, and some were fighting with their neighbors and baring their teeth.

There were even a pair of donkeys continuously braying and kicking the metal railings of their holding pen, which was causing quite a disturbance.

Needless to say, there was an awful lot of kicking and biting going on at the auction, and you had to be very careful.

We wandered closely together up and down the aisles, looking and commenting on all the horses we saw there.

Lass was clutching onto my arm, and at one point we were actually holding hands and laughing at all the strange cowpokes that had come up with their haul of horses from down south.

They seemed out of place here as they congregated with each other, leaning back against the railings with their cowboy hats tipped just over their eyes, wearing their worn out Wrangler jeans and high heeled buckaroo cowboy boots, and spitting their chewing tobacco onto the dirt floor as horses romped past them.

They had mostly come up from Texas and Oklahoma with their shipments of horses, and were waiting around for the auction to end, so that they could collect their money and return home.

As we strolled along, we suddenly came across a holding pen where there was a small black newborn colt, he was nervously pacing back and forth on his spindly long legs, and he was relentlessly whinnying, only pausing to listen for his mother to call back. He was shaking, scared and all alone.

"Sonny, that colt is too young to be on his own without his mother, he looks to be only a day old!" Lass frantically stated.

A cowboy just happened to be passing by, and I stopped him.

"Do you know what's going on with this colt, why isn't he with his mother?" I questioned.

"I do know sir, he was foaled on our way up from Oklahoma.

I heard his dam was actually once a world champion show jumper when she was younger.

She was older and out to pasture and there must have been a stud colt out there with her, and nobody figured that he was old enough to breed, and he got her pregnant.

Several months later she blew out her knee going over a jump.

The owner couldn't afford the medical bills, and I guess they didn't know that she was knocked up, let alone so close to foaling.

So they shipped her off for auction, hoping someone would have the money to fix her up.

She musta gone into labor on the way up here. The stress of shipping will do that to a horse and she went down in the trailer to give birth.

She couldn't get back up because of her blown knee, and all the other horses were trampling all over her.

She musta went into shock, and she died in the trailer.

It was a real bitch gettin' her out of there too!" The cowboy matter of factly stated.

He glanced over and noticed that Lass was tearing up as she was visibly upset.

"Sorry Mame, I don't want to seem insensitive, it's just that I see this sort of thing all the time," stated the cowboy.

"What's going to happen to him?!" exclaimed Lass.

"He already got sold to the "Grim Reaper." See that yellow tag glued to his rump that has "Hamilton" written on it.

That's Hamilton meat packing. He was so small, nobody wanted him. It's a lot of work raising a newborn foal," stated the cowboy, and he tipped his hat and continued on walking.

Lass looked up at me with her sad tearing eyes and I looked back down into hers.

We both knew in our hearts that there was no way we were going to let this poor orphaned colt die, let alone go for slaughter.

I called out to the cowboy who was now leading a limping chestnut quarter horse to the auction arena.

"Hey cowboy! Who's the Grim Reaper and where can I find him?" I sternly questioned.

"Go look in the venue stands. He'll be the weasel who looks like the devil himself, and he'll be sitting alone with a yellow flag in his hand, probably on the top row," stated the cowboy and he walked off with the limping horse in hand.

"Sonny, do you think we'll be able to save him?" Lass fearfully questioned.

"I'm not so worried about saving him, I'm more worried about keeping him alive once *you* do get him!" I simply stated.

Lass was instantly taken aback by my comment.

"You said 'YOU', Sonny?" Lass smiled.

"Hey, I'm buying him for you, this is going to be a team effort to save this little guy!" I replied.

Lass grabbed me and smothered me with kisses. She said I was definitely unlike anyone else she had ever dated before, and I could tell she was falling for me.

Together we ventured out into the auctioning venue, and visually scoured the rows of bleachers that escalated up from the wall separating the dirt floored auctioning arena.

The auctioneer was rambling on as they passed through and headed up the bleachers, ramping up the bidding on a retired gray race horse.

"Okay folks, let's start the bidding! With this horse, ladies and gentlemen you could leave home late and get to work early! Who will give me $220 for this beautiful mare? Okay here we go! $220, $225, $225 who will give me $230?" and so on, it went.

"I see him!" exclaimed Lass.

I gazed up at the countless rows of people, and sitting there on the top row, all alone, was the angel of death himself!

We proceeded to march up the bleachers, and we climbed through the crowd of seated spectators, keeping our eyes trained on him as we continued on upward in his direction.

He instantly noticed us heading his way, and he seemed to get quite uncomfortable and nervous as he observed us approaching him.

Maybe he thought we were animal activists, he obviously knows that he is the most hated man at the auction.

When we finally reached him, I sat down on one side of him and Lass on the other.

He was extremely uncomfortable and began loosening his tie.

"Are you Hamilton?" I questioned.

"I don't want any trouble from you two! I'll call security if you don't get up and leave right now!" he nervously stated.

"Never mind that, Hamilton. Here's the deal. My girlfriend wants that little black colt you have your meat hooks into," I stated.

Lass's face lit up when I referred to her as "*my girlfriend*."

Hamilton then realized that we weren't actually out to get him, and so he relaxed a bit, re-tightened his necktie, and then began to diabolically grin.

"Oh my, that's too bad for your girlfriend, maybe you should have been here earlier, and you could have out bid my one dollar bid," Hamilton chuckled.

"How much do you want for him?" demanded Sonny.

The man realizing he was holding the Aces began to think about his options.

"Ya know, they pay a lot of money in France for that baby horse veal!" Hamilton snickered.

I instantly realized this was not going to be that easy, dealing with an old experienced horse trader such as Hamilton.

"How – much – do – you – want – for – the – colt?!" I demanded.

The shrewd horse trader rubbed his face and stretched, contemplating a price for the colt.

"How much will you give me to save that colt from ending up on some Frenchmans plate?" Hamilton fiendishly questioned.

I was losing my patience, and began to make a fist, and I pulled back my arm to punch the man, when Lass stepped in.

"Hold on Sonny, Mr. Hamilton is a reasonable man and I don't think he wants his teeth knocked out over something as insignificant as a worthless colt. What my *boyfriend* is trying to say is... That skinny little malnourished foal can't be worth that much, even for meat. Don't you have any compassion left in that shriveled up pea sized stone of a heart of yours, to let us have him for a few dollars?" Lass pleaded.

The man began to hysterically laugh out loud!

"A few dollars! Didn't you ever study the economics of supply and demand in school, Missy? I have the supply and you have the demand. That means I can ask whatever I feel like for that foal.... and I'll take a hundred dollar bill for him," Hamilton roared.

Lass became frustrated, and aggressively crossed her arms.

"Okay Sonny, Go ahead and hit him!" she ordered.

The man was taken aback, and instantly changed his tone as Sonny began to once again make a fist and pull his arm back!!

"Okay, okay, give me fifty dollars and the colt is yours!" cried the old curmudgeon.

"But, you only paid a buck!" exclaimed Sonny.

"You can either pay me the fifty or go to jail for assault and battery," stated Hamilton.

I angrily reached into my pocket and pulled out a $50 bill, and crumpled it up and stuffed the money into the Grim Reaper's shirt pocket!

"That's an awwwful nice thing you're doing, Sonny. Buying that cute little colt for your girrrrlfriend," he sarcastically jeered as he wrote a receipt for the colt.

Lass stood up to leave and snatched the yellow receipt out of his creepy hand, and stared back into his black deathly eyes.

"Ya know what you are, Hamilton.... You're a real ass hole!" declared Lass.

I burst out laughing and took her by the hand to leave. Hamilton, who had been called worse things, just shrugged it off, and reached into his pocket retrieving the $50 bill and salivated, as he refolded it and then carefully stuffed it into his billfold.

Together, hand in hand we marched down the bleachers leaving Hamilton to his morbid deeds.

We quickly returned to the colt's paddock and showed the attendant the paperwork for the colt's purchase.

The colt was so weak it didn't take much to catch him, and he only weighed about 25 pounds despite his long gangly legs.

I carried him back to the truck and Lass held him on her lap the whole way home.

"I'm going to name him Ulysses!" Lass confidently stated.

"Why Ulysses?" I dumbfoundedly questioned.

Hamilton, who was the president on a ten dollar bill, bought the colt for a Washington, and you paid him with a Ulysses S. Grant!" she happily declared.

"I think that's a great name for a great colt!" I replied.

She tried to cozy up next to me as best she could with the colt on her lap, and it felt good.

We finally made it back to my farm at about midnight, and we placed the colt in a box stall that we quickly prepared in my barn.

I mixed up some powdered milk replacement formula that I had on hand, and poured it into a large nippled calf bottle.

Lass had a way with the colt, and he trusted her.

He immediately began drinking from the bottle.

"Your father is really going to be pissed at me when I bring you home tonight?" I stated.

"Who said I'm going home tonight?" she laughed.

We stayed up together all night long.

Cozied up on the fresh straw in the colts stall, holding each other, kissing and taking care of Ulysses.

Since that memorable night at the horse auction, we have never been apart, and we have been together ever since.

It was a match made in horse heaven.

Chapter 20

Approximately a year and a half later, Lass and I were married. And with the help of Lass's reluctant father, I was brought into their family construction business.

I became a farmer/developer, and it seemed that I had a certain knack for it.

I was more of a people person than my father in law, and the crews seemed to work better for me since they felt I was more down to earth and reasonable when it came to deadlines and overages.

Since Georgie had left and started his own business in Illinois, it was clear he wasn't interested in moving back to the farm.

I don't think it would have mattered anyways even if he would have come back. It didn't make monetary sense trying to save the farm, and my mother was now warming up to the idea of turning the land into a housing development.

After all, it was now all in the family, and she profited immensely from it.

After subdividing 1000 acres of the farm with my father-in-law, my mother had more money than she knew what to do with.

She gave me a portion of the old farm, which included 250 acres of land, and set aside 250 acres for Georgie to do with as he pleased.

Poor Lenny unfortunately got left out due to my fathers direct orders, and the fact that he was the family outcast.

My father stated that when he passed;

"To Lenny: I bequeath the axe he used to break poor old Sarg's leg and skull, nothing more."

I built a new home for Lass and I in the meadow where old Sarg died.

I wanted to make sure that nothing would ever disturb his resting place.

It was a sacred place where I would sit under the apple tree, and reminisce about the days I spent with him as a child.

It was nice to be able to look out from our rear porch, and see the old farm across the meadow where I grew up, and keep an eye on my mother.

I initially asked my mother to move into our new home with us. It was certainly big enough where she could have had her own area in the house.

But as old and worn as it was, she insisted on staying in the old farm house where we grew up for the rest of her life.

She said it kept her close to my father, since he had died there.

I scaled the farm down to just a few cows, some chickens and several horses.

Riding horses was Lass's passion, and Ulysses grew up to be a champion show jumper for Lass, and he was our favorite horse!

My mom still enjoyed collecting the eggs and selling them for her "spending money" as she put it, as if she needed it.

She tried to keep busy, and she had become very close with Lass. With Lass's mother gone, she managed to fill in that void and I think it meant a lot to Lass.

The farm was safer and more manageable now except for the fact that I was stuck with a very large maroon bull that I had bought several years back.

His name was "Big Red."

He was only a small calf when I bought him as a breeding bull prospect, but he turned into the biggest behemoth, son of a bitch bull anyone had ever seen!

He was now too old for slaughter, and meaner than any animal I've ever encountered.

I do believe that given the opportunity, he could kill anything on this Earth, even a grizzly bear or a rhino!

He especially hated humans, and he never forgot that it was a human that pressed that red hot branding iron onto his rump when he was weaned.

No one was interested in a bull that was so vicious and unmanageable, especially for breeding.

Not the sort of gene traits farmers wanted to pass down into their herds.

So I kept him in an extra heavy reinforced steel holding pen that was attached to the slaughterhouse.

I'm afraid that someday he might just obliterate and bust out of that steel pen and hurt someone. I really need to figure out what to do with him.

Chapter 21

Seasons passed and our family grew.

We were blessed with twins. A son and a daughter. We named our daughter after Lass's mother "June" and our son after my father "Ronald."

It was truly bliss and I enjoyed being a father more than anything.

My mother loved having the children around, and it took her mind off the absence of my father and Georgie.

It was a heartwarming event when my daughter would call out to me and say;

"Daddy…Ronny and me are going to Grandma's house," and they would run out the door holding hands, and I would watch them as they ran across the meadow to her house.

My mother would be waiting on the porch with milk and cookies, and I would know that they were safe and she loved them.

There were often times where Lass and I would saddle up our horses and each of us would take one of the kids, and plant them on the saddle in front of us, as Georgie had done with me when I was a little boy.

As we rode around the farm, I would tell the children stories of things that once were and the things we did on the farm when I was a child.

It was difficult though, to recount hardly any fond memories on the farm that I could share with the kids, especially how terrible it was with Lenny around.

For the most part, all that I told them about Lenny was that he was a no good rotten brother.

"Lenny the loser" we called him, and the kids would boo and turn their thumbs down and hold their noses whenever his name was mentioned.

I often wondered whatever became of Lenny.

Maybe I feared that he might return to the farm one day.

It's funny that even though I am a grown man and I know I can handle him, he still scares the shit out of me.

I always thought that possibly he was either wasting away in some prison or riding the tail gate of a garbage truck somewhere, complaining about me to whomever was there to listen to him.

Either way, I was glad he wasn't in my life anymore.

If Georgie hadn't run him off when he did, I do believe that at some point he would have arranged a fatal accident to kill me, so that he could reclaim his position in the family hierarchy that he was so angered about losing when I was born.

Chapter 22

Years had gone by, and Lenny continued working for Sedone and his gang.

The promise of making him a "rich man" after he had saved Sedones life never really materialized, but he did enjoy his work and he felt that these low-lifes and slugs were his family now.

After all, beating and killing people was what Lenny enjoyed most, and so did they.

Occasionally, Lenny was paired up with one of Sedones less sinister thugs named Billy Sparks.

Billy was the black man in the lineup that night, when Lenny first showed up at Sedones restaurant, and saved them all from being executed by Bobby G's gang.

He was a handsome, suave and debonair black man from New York City, who preferred to wear bright colored suits to the dark ominous ones the rest of the gang wore.

He was a gifted ladies man, and above all, style was his foremost objective.

He had a string of women from Chicago to… well Billy had women everywhere.

He was a bit of a philosopher and a gifted gabber who loved to hear himself talk, and the women loved his confident stature and his charisma.

Lenny and Billy were relaxing in a car, drinking coffee and smoking as they were preparing for their next collection one morning.

"Okay, we've been sitting around long enough. Let's go collect some dead presidents," ordered Lenny.

Billy stretched back into the driver's seat and drifted off into one of his moments while taking a long drag from his cigarette.

"Let me tell you a story, Lenny. And I want you to pay attention... One summer day, when I was a young boy, I laid on the cool green grass in my front yard and looked way up at the sky.

As I laid there, I reached up and I decided that I wanted to touch it.

I got up, jumped up and down, but I was too short and I couldn't reach it!

Then I hopped up on the roof of my dad's car, but I was still too short to touch the sky.

I noticed that there was a big old willow tree next to my house and it seemed to touch the sky, so I started climbing up that tree. I don't know how I did it, but I remember getting up to the top of that tree, but I still couldn't touch the sky. There was a limb that stretched over to the edge of the roof of my house, I looked down and saw that I was over 2 stories up! I wasn't giving up so I shimmied over on that branch and hopped onto the roof of my house! I began climbing up the tall and steep incline to the peak of the roof, and I was thinking that I would definitely be able to get my hands on some of that sky from up there.

When I finally made it all the way up to the top of the peak, I was even more disappointed that I still couldn't touch it!

It was then that I realized that the sky was much higher than I originally thought, and maybe it wasn't meant for touchin'. Unfortunately, now I was stuck 3 stories up on the roof with no way to get down!" stated Billy.

"So what happened?" yawned Lenny.

"I started cryin' and screaming my head off until a neighbor finally saw me sitting on the peak of my roof!! I was hangin' onto the TV antenna for dear life, and bawling my eyes out!

He called my momma, and she came runnin' outside thinkin' it was a joke, until she saw me stuck up there!

She started cussin' me out, and yellin' at me that she was gonna give me an ass whoopin' that I would never forget, when I got down!

She called the fire department, and they sent a fire truck over with a power ladder on it to get me off the roof.

The whole neighborhood came out to see what was goin' on!

When they finally got me to the ground, I tried to make a run for it, but my momma grabbed my ass before I could get away.

It was so embarrassin' since she pulled my pants down all the way, including my boxers, and she commenced beatin' my skinny bare ass in front of the whole neighborhood!

All the folks were laughin' at me and calling me 'Dumbo the Flyin' Elephant!'" Billy exclaimed.

"Is this story almost over?" inquired Lenny.

"Would you like to know what the moral of the story is?" asked Billy.

"Uhmm, you gotta have big elephant ears to fly?" replied Lenny.

"No Fool!! It's don't be a dumb ass, and go after things that are out of your reach! Right now you are one of Sedones pigeons, and that's what you are always going to be. You are never gonna be the boss," exclaimed Billy.

"So are you gonna be the boss?" sarcastically questioned Lenny.

"Listen man, I am the best that ever was...and I ain't never got caught! Even Sedone never caught me," exclaimed Billy.

"Caught you at what?" Lenny asked, puzzled.

"Whatever you can think of man, I was never caught! Now shut up and get out of the car. I have to go meet a lady!" ordered Billy.

"What lady are you meeting up with?" questioned Lenny.

"The one that I never got caught with, fool!" shouted Billy.

"What about collecting the dough?" questioned Lenny.

"I'll be back after lunch, we'll do it then," replied Billy.

Lenny shook his head in disbelief and hesitantly got out of the car.

"Sparks, you may be the best that ever was, but if you keep it up, you're gonna get caught, and your wife's gonna kill your cheatin' ass!!" Lenny professed.

Billy gave him the finger and loudly laughed as he sped off.

With nothing else to do Lenny decided to make some rounds, and he did a bit of collecting on his own. He began thinking about his future and the fact that he would always be one of Sedone's pigeons, and never make the big money like his boss unless he made some changes.

"One day I'm gonna make my move on Sedone, and take over Chicago. Then I'll be sitting pretty with my own gang of hoodlums and loads of cash. My time is coming soon," Lenny surmised.

Chapter 23

The following morning Sedone had called both Lenny and Billy into his office for a "Board" meeting.

Typically it was to inform the men about collection and debt redemptions from specific clients.

It was rare that anyone was able to finally settle up with Sedone and finish paying off their debts. It was inevitable for the most part, that once you were under Sedones thumb, you were never going to squeeze out from underneath it. Sedone had a way of accruing interest that made his loans impossible to pay off.

That's how he made his money, and that's why he liked having Lenny around.

Sedone loved money and Lenny loved shaking people down for it.

"Gentlemen, I have an outstanding balance from a certain pezza di nerda (piece of crap). He had borrowed a large sum of money to start a business a few years back, and after all the kindness I had bestowed on him, he doesn't want to pay his interest or his debt back anymore. I need you two to go talk to him, and make him understand that it's not nice to ask for my help, and then insult the feelings of your friend that helped you get started," Sedone commanded.

"Do you want us to give him something to remind him, like a broken arm or a busted jaw?" matter of factly, questioned Lenny.

"You always want to kick somebody's ass Lenny, let's just go talk to the dude, we can always go back and bust his ass up at a later time," Billy sternly stated.

"Go on you two, and don't come back without some money," ordered Sedone.

And he slipped a piece of paper with the name and address of the man to Billy.

"How much does he owe?" inquired Lenny.

"He started out with a $5,000 loan, and he paid me back all of it. But he still owes me the compounding interest of about $12,000 large," snickered Sedone.

"Oh, this is going to be fun!" Lenny salivated as they walked out the back door of the pizza restaurant and hopped into Billy's car.

Billy started the car as Lenny settled into the passenger seat.

"How come we never heard of this deal before now? And who's been collecting the payments?" Lenny questioned.

"Either Sedone was doing it himself to stay in shape, or one of the other guys, I guess?" said Billy, and they drove off.

Chapter 24

Billy recklessly drove his car through the busy streets of Chicago towards the outskirts of the city.

They traversed through the streets for almost 40 minutes of seemingly aimless driving.

"Where the hell is this place!?" complained Lenny.

Billy glanced again at the address.

"It's in the "good" side of town, and not the usual type of neighborhood we are accustomed to," replied Billy.

"What was the name of this place we are going to, again?" Lenny impatiently inquired.

"It's right over there in that block of buildings; 'Georgie's TV and Radio Barn'," replied Billy in his country western accent.

"That's funny, I had a brother named Georgie. I haven't seen that piece of shit since I beat the livin' pulp out of him about 15 years ago, back home in Binghamton.

And, on account of that beating, my parents kicked me off the farm," remarked Lenny.

"Brotherly love, Lenny, brotherly love," replied Billy.

"Yeah, brotherly love my ass, if it wasn't for him and my little brother Sonny, I would be sitting pretty right now!" exclaimed Lenny.

"What did your little brother do to mess you up?" inquired Billy.

"He was born, and I was screwed!" sternly replied Lenny.

"Do you know anything about the Bible, Lenny?" Billy questioned.

"Yeah, I know it's a good place to hide a gun if you cut out the pages!" chuckled Lenny.

"Okay Milkweed, now I'm gonna teach you something else. All through the ages, according to the Bible there has been family conflict. This cat named Cain whacked his brother Abel with a rock, because he was jealous of him. A bunch of other brothers who hated their little brother Joseph, tossed him down into a well to get rid of him, because they felt like crap on account of their old man played him as his favorite! Dear old Dad, gave Joseph a psychedelic colored robe and they all got goat shit! They were jealous dudes, just like you!" exclaimed Billy.

"Yeah that sounded like my life on the farm. I would have enjoyed knocking off my older brother with a rock to the head and throwing my little brat brother down the well to get rid of them both!" reminisced Lenny.

"Don't you see that jealousy is the poison that destroys everything Lenny? Family, friends, people you work with, and especially women!" proclaimed Billy.

Lenny just sat there looking out the window and listened, and then he turned to Billy.

"So does that mean you are jealous of me, Billy?" Lenny smirked.

"Ya, I wish I had all your dough and beautiful women, you moron!" Billy chuckled.

It seemed that Billy had struck a chord with Lenny, and it brought Lenny back to a time in his youth where he felt that he was treated unfairly by his family. His blood began to boil inside of him as he reminisced his final night at the farm, and the beating his brother Georgie had given him.

His only regret was that he had left so abruptly that night, that he wasn't able to get the money he had stolen from Georgie's safe, since it was stashed in his room, in a hole in his mattress.

If he had that money he wouldn't have had to rob the gas station, and therefore he never would have gotten pinched by that cop and wound up in jail. Another reason to blame his family for his demise.

It was Georgie's fault that he couldn't get at the money he had stolen from him.

Chapter 25

Billy's car abruptly halted in front of the store.

There were dozens of color television's playing and stereo equipment showcased behind the large windows of the store front.

Billy suggested that he would go in and do the talking, and Lenny should wait outside and be available if needed.

"I thought I was going to get to break an arm or something!" complained Lenny.

"Hold on tweety, let me just see how this cat's going to meow before you go stomp on his tail," said Billy.

They both got out of the car and Lenny lit up a cigarette and leaned against the front fender of the car as Billy went into the store.

After a few minutes, there was some commotion and shouting coming from the store, and Billy quickly came running out and returned to the car!

"So what happened?! Did you get the dough?!" asked Lenny.

"That cracker is big…real big! He told me to get the hell out of his store and he started swinging his Louisville slugger bat! We better go back and get a few more guys for this one, Lenny! That guy was one big bastard!" exclaimed Billy.

"Wait here, let me go in and talk to this putz! I'll teach him a lesson and show him who he's dealing with! Besides, Sedone ain't going to like it if we come back with our tails between our legs and empty handed," exclaimed Lenny.

"Go ahead man, but I don't want you getting any of your honky blood all over my nice clean car seats on the way to the hospital...Got it man?" insisted Billy.

"Get in the car Billy, I'll be out in a few minutes," stated Lenny and he reached into the back seat of the car, and grabbed a sawed off shotgun that was laying on the back seat!

Lenny then marched to the entrance of the store and kicked the door open with such force, it almost ripped it off its hinges!

Chapter 26

Lenny was surrounded by dozens of televisions and radios loudly blaring in the store.

Each television set had the same channel tuned in, and every radio was set to the Cubs baseball game.

Then, from out of the back stockroom, a very large angry man charged out, and he was carrying a wooden baseball bat!

"Who the hell do you think you are busting in here like that?!" shouted the merchant as he charged toward Lenny, swinging his baseball bat!

Lenny in turn charged towards the merchant brandishing his sawed-off shotgun!

"You're going to pay up sucker or I'm gonna blow your head off!" shouted Lenny.

Suddenly the two angry men were face to face with each other and in total shock!

They both were staring and squinting at each other in disbelief, as they both suddenly recognized one another!

"Lenny??... Is that you?" stunningly questioned Georgie.

"Georgie??...What the hell are you doing here?!" Lenny exclaimed.

The two brothers lowered their weapons, and dumbfoundedly looked each other over for the moment.

So much time had passed and both were much older and different looking now.

It wasn't a joyful reunion, no hugging, in fact not even a hand shake. Neither brother had forgotten the past, and as far as Lenny was concerned, he still had a score to settle with Georgie.

"After you left we didn't know what happened to you," proclaimed Georgie.

"Ya mean after I left the joint. Yeah, I bet you were all worried sick about me," Lenny sarcastically stated.

Georgie just shrugged his shoulders awkwardly in response.

"So how's Mom and the Old Man?" questioned Lenny.

"Sorry to say Lenny, but Dad died a few years back. The smoking finally caught up with him.

Mom had a hard time with Dad's passing and she put Sonny up on this gigantic pedestal. Whenever I would call her, all she would do is brag about how wonderful Sonny was!

He took over the farm and hooked up with a rich land developer's daughter. That son of a bitch subdivided 1000 acres of our farm and built houses all over it. He made a fortune while I'm sitting here nickel and diming it, and in debt over my head! It's not fair! I was supposed to get the farm! Not him!

Then to add insult to injury, he stole what was left of the farm from Mom! The whole barn setup and all the farm equipment, along with 250 acres of land!

He's letting mom rot away in our old junky house, but I bet that cheap bastard is charging her rent!

He's married now and has two little twin kids, and he built himself a fancy mansion right in Sarg's pasture!" stated Georgie.

When the name Sarg came up, the tension rose, and it became uncomfortable for both brothers as it rekindled the event that changed both their lives. And it just so happened that Georgie failed to mention the fact that he also received 250 acres of the farm as well, and all that was left to Lenny was the ax.

"So, Sonny is sitting pretty on our land? He probably tricked Mom into signing everything over to him," sneered Lenny.

"Yeah, you're probably right, he tricked her!" replied Georgie.

"So Georgie, you really got yourself in a jam here. You never should have gotten mixed up with Sedone, he's never gonna let you off the hook for the dough. No matter how much you pay him back. That's how he operates. He sent us here to bust you up, and collect some of the money you owe him," stated Lenny.

"I had no choice, I kept asking Sonny to loan me some money to get me on my feet, and he kept telling me "No." He said that if he gave me the loan, I would never talk to him again because of the money," complained Georgie.

"I don't know Georgie, you got yourself in a real mess. I'm supposed to get some dough out of you or bring back a finger or something to Sedone," stated Lenny.

Georgie was taken aback by Lenny's remark and began to get nervous.

"Isn't there something you can do to help me, Lenny? Can you please talk to Sedone and tell him I'm your big brother, your family, and to give me a break? We're brothers Lenny, and I love you! Please Lenny, I'm begging you to help me, brother!" groveled Georgie.

"Lenny just stood there motionless, and watched as Georgie begged and cried for his help.

"Okay, sure Georgie, you leave it to me. I'll get you off the hook with Sedone. After all we're brothers, and blood is thicker than water, right Georgie?" grinned Lenny.

Just then Billy Sparks cautiously popped his head in through the open door.

"Everything alright here, Lenny?" questioned Billy.

"Yeah, I was just finishing up here, we reached an agreement," smugly stated Lenny.

"You better have the dough tonight or you'll be limping around with a broken leg tomorrow!" scolded Lenny and he smiled and winked at Georgie.

As the two thugs left the store, Lenny gave Georgie a "Thumbs up" behind his back as they left.

Lenny tossed the shotgun back into the back seat, and then they jumped into Billy's car and sped away.

"Do you think he's going to come up with the money?" asked Billy.

"I had a long talk with that stooge, and I explained to the big goof that if he doesn't come up with some dough tonight, I'm gonna have to chop off a few of his fingers!

He said he needed his fingers to play the piano, so he promised me that he would have either the cash or something really valuable for me tonight," stated Lenny.

"Okay, but you are gonna have to report back to Sedone that we collected nothin', and work it out with him that you are coming back later. I have a date tonight," stated Billy.

They continued on back to Sedones and Lenny couldn't stop thinking about the odds of running into his brother Georgie in Chicago.

Suddenly Billy slammed on the brakes, and his car screeched to a halt, thrusting Lenny forward into the dashboard.

They were at an intersection, and still about 20 blocks away from Sedones.

"What the hell just happened!" Lenny exclaimed

"Get out here, I just saw a pretty girl on the sidewalk and she smiled at me, fool!" shouted Billy.

"What are you talkin' about! You don't even know her!" exclaimed Lenny.

"Hurry up and get out before she gets away!" shouted Billy.

"Can't you just drop me off in front of the restaurant you horny bastard?" Lenny complained.

"No fool! Now hurry up and beat it!" Billy scorned.

Lenny shook his head in disbelief and got out of the car, and gave him the finger as Billy sped off and pulled over along the sidewalk.

"Hey! I like your smile you beautiful goddess, what's your name baby?" he heard Billy shouting out from down the street.

Chapter 27

As Lenny sauntered down the busy sidewalk, he began to get heated up after his surprise encounter with Georgie.

He couldn't go back to the restaurant empty handed, and explain to Sedone why he didn't have his money. So Lenny decided it would be better to just walk back to his apartment and figure things out.

As he walked on, the chance encounter of his meeting up with Georgie began stirring up memories of the old farm, and they were bad memories for Lenny.

Even though Lenny made everyone's life on the farm miserable, Lenny believed that in fact he was the victim, and it was everyone else that caused him the anguish.

It festered in him as he relived the night Georgie beat him to a pulp, and the way he was pushed aside after Sonny was born.

The day his father beat him when he found him in the milk room with Eddie. And how his mother never stood up for him, and always coddled Sonny.

It was always;

"Lenny! Leave Sonny alone, he's just a baby! Lenny, I'm taking care of Sonny, go do your homework! Lenny, Lenny, Lenny. Blah, blah, blah!" Lenny scoffed.

The only one who he felt ever gave a damn about him was Eddie, and his father killed him!

His anger raged as it was fueled by his memories, and it began to consume him.

"I can't let those bastards get away with what they did to me, it's not in my nature to forgive and forget," he whispered as he ground his teeth in anger.

As he marched on, he contrived a maniacal plan in his devious mind to get revenge for what his family had done to him.

"I'm going to teach those bastards back in Binghampton a lesson they'll never forget! When I'm done with them, they'll wish they never disrespected me!" he maniacally thought.

Every step he took, his plan became more and more diabolical. He was going to take back all that was his. With everyone dead, he would be the final heir to the farm. And now that he had a plan, there was only one thing on his mind…Pay back!

Chapter 28

Lenny finally arrived at his run down antiquated apartment building, and drudged up the 8 flights of stairs to his apartment.

Despite Sedones promises of fame and fortune, Lenny was living a modest existence, while his boss was wealthy and living uptown in a big fancy house.

Lenny's apartment was small and dingy. The only furniture he had was a twin sized bed, a bureau and an old black and white TV.

The filthy kitchen sink was full of dirty dishes and silverware that had been neglected for many weeks, and the apartment was infested with rodents and cockroaches.

Lenny entered his kitchen area and removed a metal strong box which was hidden in the cabinet underneath the sink.

When he opened the box, the remembrances and souvenirs he collected that night he killed Big Al were all in there.

The large diamond ring, the fancy engraved chrome and ivory handled pistol and the stacks of money that he had taken. Even "Frank the Indians" finger was still floating around in that pickle jar, and the crumbled up photograph of Sedone in front of his pizza restaurant. It was all in there, in that heinous time capsule, just waiting for Lenny to reopen it.

He gathered up some clothes and threw them into his old duffle bag, which still contained his machine gun and a few drums of ammunition.

He stuffed the diamond ring into his shirt pocket and placed the chrome gun behind his back, then he put on a jacket and left his apartment, grabbing a half empty bottle of Cutty Sark whiskey, and the carton of cigarettes off his bureau on his way out.

He marched down the 8 flights of stairs to the street, and used a payphone on the street corner to call Sedone.

The phone rang once, and Sedone immediately picked it up.

"Hey Sedone, it's me, Lenny," he matter of factly stated.

"Minga! Where have you been?! I was waiting here all day to find out what happened with the TV guy, you bastardo!" exclaimed Sedone.

"Don't get excited Sedone, Billy got chased out of the shop by the big slug, and so I went in and we had it out.

By the time I was done with the big meathead he was puddy in my hands. He swore to me on his mother's life that he will have something for you tonight," surmised Lenny.

"If I got a pound of mozzarella cheese every time someone swore to me on their mother's life, and then they stiffed me, I could open a pizza restaurant!" shouted Sedone

"Sedone you have a pizza restaurant," replied Lenny.

"That's right you idiot!" shouted Sedone.

"Don't worry, Sedone. I'm going back to the TV guy right now to squeeze him some more. I'll come by later with the money," stated Lenny.

"Lenny, wait hold on, I think you are going to need help.

I'm sending Dante over to go with you. I don't think this guy is going to pay up so easily, and I don't want you to get your ass kicked by this big ape. It will be embarrassing for us if that happens. Dante is going with you to back you up!" insisted Sedone.

Dante was Sedone's notorious hitman nephew. He was a cold as steel merciless killer in his mid thirties, who resembled the actor Charles Bronson. He was ruthless and he made an efficient sport out of killing people.

Dante was actually much worse and even more maniacal than Lenny, if that was even possible!

But his demeanor was different from Lennys. He was extremely intimidating, and intense. His fierce stare was usually enough to frighten most people into submission, and murdering for him was as comfortable as blowing out a match.

His persona was slow, stiff and rigid, hardened and emotionless, and he rarely revealed any emotions other than gloating about how he heinously made his victims suffer during his countless kills.

"No thanks, Sedone! With no disrespect to Dante, I can handle this on my own. If the guy doesn't cough up the dough, then you can send in Dante. Besides I'm almost at the guys place," stated Lenny.

"Okay Lenny, have it your way, but come right back here when you are done, and you had better not screw this up!" shouted Sedone and he hung up the phone.

Lenny ground his teeth and paused as he held the phone and thought of the days his father would utter those same endearing words to him;

"Lenny you screwed it up!" He couldn't control his anger and became enraged and began smashing the pay phone to pieces and left the broken receiver dangling by its metal cord.

He marched around the corner into a nearby alley where his car was parked. It was a green 1957 chevy Belair that Sedone had recently given to him as a gift of appreciation.

As he approached his car he noticed it was covered with dozens of parking tickets.

He frivolously pulled them off his windshield and tossed them into the street.

"Yeah, like I'm seriously gonna pay these," he laughed to himself.

He unlocked the door and it creaked loudly as he opened the heavy door, and he tossed his duffle bag onto the back seat.

When he put the key into the ignition, the engine hesitated a moment, but then quickly turned over and started.

He felt hungry, and since all of the excitement of running into his older brother that morning, he realized he hadn't eaten all day.

He decided he needed to kill some time and what better way than to have a nice leisurely sit down supper before he returned to Sedones.

And so he drove over to his favorite restaurant in the Chinatown district of Chicago.

The narrow streets were completely occupied by parked cars and there was no street parking available.

Lenny, who makes his own rules to suit himself, pulled in through a narrow gap between two parked cars and drove over the curb and onto the sidewalk, and parked his car facing the front of a small Asian restaurant called "The Mandarin Junk," totally blocking the pedestrian sidewalk traffic with his car. The restaurant was unusually busy for that time of the day, and Lenny marched right past the snobby hostess and continued on to the back of the restaurant, and he sat himself down at a massive corner booth table which was marked "reserved."

The mortified restaurant owner immediately approached Lenny, and offered him a smaller table, since he was all alone, as he desperately needed that table for an affluent party of twelve, who would be arriving there at any minute. Lenny arrogantly ignored him and wouldn't budge, and he just calmly sat there and lit up a cigarette as he patiently waited for his waitress.

The frustrated owner finally gave up and barked several derogatory Chinese words at him, and threw up his hands and walked away.

Although Lenny was a familiar patron there, he was always considered a loner and would only order frugally off of the modest combination menu.

No one really knew much about him other than he was a cheapskate.

Little did they know that Lenny was a cold blooded killer who worked for the very mob that they were paying their protection money too.

There was another significant reason why Lenny favored this restaurant. There was a pretty Asian waitress who worked there, who had caught Lenny's eye.

Her name was "Sue Chinn" and Lenny, out of character, had fallen in love with her.

When she noticed Lenny, she immediately darted over and greeted him with a hot cup of tea.

She knew Lenny was courting her, since he was at the restaurant at least 4 times a week and always flirted with her.

She was most likely hoping to be rescued from her menial job at the restaurant, and oddly she was beginning to have an affinity towards him too. She always smiled at him, but unfortunately she could barely speak much English, and she would just shake her head up and down and laugh at whatever he said to her.

"Sue, did I ever tell you how much I dislike pizza? My freakin' boss owns a pizza joint and he once told me that I could eat all the pizza I wanted there... problem is, I hate his frigging pizza!" he sarcastically stated to her.

She always giggled and seemed to agree with whatever he was saying, and then quickly walked off to get him a menu.

When she returned, she smiled and handed him the menu, with a note and her phone number scribbled on it.

Lenny was pleasantly surprised and told her (basically in sign language), that he was going away for a few days, but they would get together, when he returned.

She giddily leaned over and passionately kissed him on the mouth and quickly ran off to the kitchen.

Lenny was very excited, considering most women despised him. And now, he was finally on his way to having a real girlfriend, and possibly someone who seemed to actually care about him.

Things seemed to be finally looking up and falling into place for Lenny.

As he glanced over the menu, a woman heading toward the restroom had passed by his table wearing a strong perfume.

It instantly triggered him to suddenly reflect back to the incident at Grand Central Station, when he left his duffle bag unattended, and it was stolen right out from under his nose.

He suddenly realized that once again he had left his duffle bag unattended, but this time it was in his car, and in a neighborhood that it was likely to get stolen again.

He quickly jumped out of the booth, and ran out to retrieve the bag from his car!

When he passed through the restaurant's front door, he noticed that there was an agitated motorcycle policeman standing beside his car, and a tow truck had just arrived and was preparing to hook up and tow his car away.

"Whoa officer, I just stopped by to pick up an order of take out!" Lenny exclaimed.

"Too bad, you should have parked down the street in the parking lot. Illegally parking on the sidewalk is going to get you a $50 ticket and your car towed! And when I looked up your plate number, I found that you owe $4,800 in back parking violations. What do you think, you own the road or something, wise guy? After you pay all your fines, you can pick up your car at the impound lot," coarsely stated the police officer, and he continued writing out another parking violation to add to Lenny's collection.

Lenny was ready to blow a fuse and was beside himself!

In the first place, most of all those outstanding fines were from when Sedone owned the car!

"Gee thanks, Sedone!" he thought to himself.

This was really throwing a giant monkey wrench in his whole scheme, and after everything was going so well for him today!

"Officer, I need to get my duffle bag out of the car before you tow it away," pleaded Lenny.

"Sorry Mister, access denied until you pay off all your past due fines!" scolded the officer.

"But Officer, I can't pay the fines without the money in the duffle bag!" Lenny exclaimed.

"Hmmm, that's a problem, but it's not my problem, it's your problem! Now step aside and go eat your Chinese takeout food, you lazy bastard," chuckled the officer.

That was the final straw.

Lenny couldn't contain himself anymore and the situation triggered him to resolve the issue the only way he knew how, violently.

He instinctively reached behind his back, and drew out Big Al's big fancy chrome gun, and in that same stride he spontaneously fired the gun and shot the officer in the chest, knocking him over the hood of his car!

The loud bang jarred the attention of the tow truck driver, who immediately threw his hands up and began slowly backing away from Lenny's car!

Lenny pulled the trigger again and shot the man in the head, killing him instantly and he fell backward and collapsed against the back of his tow truck!

He then heard a witness's horrific scream coming from inside the restaurant, and when he quickly turned to see who it was, he saw that it was Sue Chinn! She was standing there horrified, with her hands intensely clutching the sides of her face, as she had just witnessed Lenny murdering two people as she stood in the doorway of the restaurant!

He coldly raised his arm and aimed his gun at her, and then pulled the trigger, shooting her directly through her heart, and he killed her instantly!

Lenny then raced over to the driver's side door, fumbled with his keys, and while doing so, he leaned down toward the dead policeman, and shouted "Who are you calling a Lazy Bastard, you Ass Hole!!" and then he jumped in and started his car.

However he was now blocked in by the tow truck and the restaurant!

He recklessly put his car in reverse and floored his accelerator, and then crashed into the back of the tow truck, knocking it forward several feet!

He was then able to turn his car just enough where he was able to maneuver forward, and then he swung his car around, and smashed his way through a narrow gap between a parked car and a fire hydrant and he sped off, leaving parts of his car and a bloody trail of death behind him.

He swiftly careened through the city streets as he made his getaway, and regretfully thought a moment about Sue Chinn, but blamed her for her own demise, and that it was her own fault that he had to kill her.

"If only she kept her nose out of my business! that stupid broad," he thought to himself.

But ultimately she ended up like most others who were involved with Lenny, blamed and dead.

Chapter 29

It was just past 6 PM at Sedone's pizza restaurant, when Lenny smugly sauntered into Sedone's office.

Sedone was counting a stack of money, as his nephew Dante sat on a couch cleaning his fingernails with a switchblade knife, and he immediately zeroed in on Lenny with his pulverizing icy cold stare as he strolled in.

Lenny made sure not to make eye contact with Dante, but reached out to shake his hand, which Dante ignored.

Sedone reluctantly got up, and hugged Lenny and kissed his cheek.

"So Lenny, how did you make out? Where's the money?!" exclaimed Sedone.

"Well Sedone, here's how it went down with that big ape. When I showed up, the guy was hiding in the back room. I had to go back there and rough him up a lot when he told me he didn't have any of the dough," reported Lenny.

"Minga, what the fazool...don't tell me you got nothing from that big ox!" exclaimed Sedone.

"Hold on Sedone, give me a chance to tell you what happened," replied Lenny.

"I knew this was not going to go so good! You should have taken Dante with you, like I told you!" Sedone barked.

"Relax Sedone, let me talk. So he didn't have any of the money, but after a lot of persuasion he finally had enough of the beating I was giving him. He said that he had something valuable that he could give me to settle his debt with you, and he started staggering over toward his desk and opened a drawer. At first I thought he was going for a gun, and I quickly drew on the oaf. But he held up his hands and slowly reached into the desk drawer, and picked up and handed an impressive piece of jewelry over to me."

"We are all squared up, and my debt with Sedone is over. This ring is worth a hundred times more than what I owed Sedone!" the lug stated.

Sedone and Dante listened intently as Lenny bragged, but they both were getting impatient, and had low expectations that Lenny actually had pulled anything off.

Lenny then reached down into his shirt pocket and removed Big Al's large diamond ring, and handed it to Sedone.

"Minga Dante!!! Look at the size of this diamond!" Sedone gasped.

Lenny ignorantly watched on as he had just lit the fuse to a 1000 megaton powder keg, and he just stood back and waited for the fireworks to begin.

Sedone examined the ring, and after a moment of jubilation, his face began to contort as he read the inscription inside the ring.

"Lenny you got this from that TV guy?" questioned Sedone.

Sedone tossed the ring to Dante, and after he inspected it, he tossed it back to Sedone.

"Yeah Sedone, he went on to say that he lifted it off a slug when he was down and out in New York City about 13 years ago," stated Lenny.

"Lenny, do you have any idea who this ring belonged to?" questioned Sedone as he was becoming enraged.

"The guy Georgie ripped off in New York City. I guess it's a pretty valuable piece of jewelry, so I did good, right boss?" proclaimed Lenny.

Sedone became increasingly agitated as he inspected the ring.

"Lenny, can you read what it says inside this ring?" Sedone asked.

Lenny was playing stupid and squinted as he tried to read the engraving.

"Gee Sedone, I don't know, can I borrow your glasses?" asked Lenny.

"Never mind Lenny…It says, "My Brother's Keeper." I recognize this ring, because it belonged to my brother, Alberto! The engraving means we look out for each other!

Whoever had this ring was the person who killed my brother, Alberto!" scorned Sedone.

"That Georgie guy must have been the guy who knocked off your brother, Alberto! So, I guess I did good, Sedone?" pestered Lenny.

"Lenny, you are like a son to me. Yes you did good!" replied Scdone.

Sedone placed the ring on his finger and made a fist.

"Dante get the car and let's go get this Georgie guy! He's going to pay for what he has done to my brother!" insisted Sedone.

"Uhh, Sedone as much as I'd like to join in on the fun, would it be okay if I took off for a few days to go visit my old lady back at the farm.

It's her birthday tomorrow and I'd like to show up and really give her the surprise of her life?" said Lenny.

Sedone paused.

"Go ahead, and here's a few bucks! Go and buy her something nice for her birthday, you earned it today, Lenny!" affirmed Sedone, and he slapped a single bill into his hand. Lenny glanced down and felt appreciated when he noticed the digits 1 and 0 on the money, and thought it was a hundred dollar bill, but then quickly realized it was just a measly ten dollar bill!

"Gee thanks Sedone, I'll make sure to write your name on her birthday card," sarcastically replied Lenny.

The back door swung open, and Billy had just wandered in and asked what was going on?

"It's Showtime," Dante coolly replied.

Sedone jumped up and grabbed his hat, trench coat and a machine gun.

"We have some important business to take care of Billy, go get my limo you're coming with us," ordered Sedone.

Sedone and Dante went out the back door when they saw Billy arrive with the car.

They both jumped into the back seat, and they sped away into the night.

"That'll teach you to mess with me, Georgie. You're going to have a real good beatin' this evenin'! Only it's going to be a lot worse than the one I got the night you beat the crap out of me! The difference is, I managed to get away, and live. Tonight, you're going to die a horrible death my brother, and pay the price for what you did to me! Consider the score even!" Lenny ghoulishly snickered.

Lenny picked up his hat and headed off to his car.

"Next stop...Binghamton, New York!" he uttered under his breath.

Chapter 30

Sedone's Limo tires screeched on the black pavement as Billy sped through the streets of Chicago!
They were on their way to avenge the death of Sedones' brother.

"Where am I drivin' to Sedone?" questioned Billy.

"Just drive to that Georgie guy's TV store, he has an apartment above it.

Thanks to Lenny, he solved the mystery of who killed my brother Alberto in New York City. It was that guy, and I'm gonna kill that son a ma bitch! Then we are going to dump him in the lake for the eels to eat through his body!" growled Sedone.

Dante sat quietly, in deep thought as he sat next to Sedone, cocking and uncocking the hammer on his large caliber pistol.

"Ya know Sedone, not for nothin', but somethin' don't smell right about this whole ring deal. Doesn't it seem strange that nobody could get squat out of this guy Georgie for months? Then Lenny the stoonade shows up, and he claims to shake down the big gorilla, and all on his own. And then he goes back to the guys' store all by himself with no back up, and does another shake down on the big ox, only this time he claims to have given him the beatin' of his life?! Then suddenly the big slug couldn't take scrawny Lenny's pounding any more, and so he caves in and springs the giant rock that he's been supposedly sittin' on all this time. And it just so happens to be Uncle Alberto's ring!

Sedone, Lenny said the guy got it when he was "down and out" in New York City, but Lenny was from New York too.

Before we take this guy out, I think we should keep our cool and see what he has to say about the whole ring thing...we can always kill his ass after," remarked Dante.

"Okay Dante, you're right, let's find out what's going on, it's possible something stinks, especially when Lenny is involved," replied Sedone.

The car approached Georgies store and they drove around back, and screeched to a halt.

The three men jumped out of the car and headed towards the back door of the building.

It was locked, but they could hear that Georgie was upstairs in his apartment talking on the phone.

Billy jimmied the door with a pocket knife, and the three men stealthily tip-toed up the staircase leading up to Georgie's apartment.

They stood there holding their breath and waited quietly as they listened outside the door, and overheard Georgie speaking to his mother on the phone.

"Yeah Ma, I couldn't believe it when I came walking out of my office, and saw Lenny come barging into my store! He is mixed up with some really bad guys, Ma. Killers, mobsters and loan sharks. He hasn't changed one bit though, a real piece of crap, Ma. Scum of the earth," Georgie rambled.

Georgie then wished his mother a happy birthday and hung up the phone.

"You are right my nephew, something's going on here," Sedone whispered to Dante.

"Surprise, Lenny told me on the way to the TV shop that he had a brother named Georgie, and they had a real bad falling out with each other.

Holy shit Sedone, this guy Georgie must be Lenny's brother!" whispered Billy.

Sedone became anxious and took the butt of his gun and tapped it three times against the door.

"Who's there?!!" nervously barked Georgie.

Instantly, Dante lifted his foot and kicked the door in, and the three men were suddenly standing there in the doorway, aiming their guns at Georgie!

Georgie was terrified as he stood there in his underwear, and searched desperately for a possible escape route, but the three men had him cornered and he had nowhere to run to.

"Sit down Georgie. Relax, I just want to talk to you," stated Sedone calmly.

"I told you before, I don't have any more money Sedone! I paid you back all the money I borrowed from you and more!" cried Georgie.

"Relax Godzilla, the boss just wants to talk to you, and then we'll be on our way, it's not about the money," said Billy.

Georgie was forcefully pushed down by Dante onto a wooden kitchen armchair while Sedone circled around him.

"So Georgie, you came from New York City a few years ago, and I have something that I want to ask you about," stated Sedone.

He made a fist with the ring on his finger, and placed it in front of Georgie's face.

"Where did you get this diamond ring from?!!" demanded Sedone.

Dante stood in front of him presenting his ice cold stare, never breaking eye contact with Georgie's eyes as Billy kept his revolver trained on him.

"Sedone, I never saw that ring before in my life! I don't know what you are talking about?!" stammered Georgie.

"Listen to me wise guy, Billy came to see you this morning and you chased him out of your store, and then another one of my guys came in, do you remember that?" drilled Sedone.

"Of course I remember that, it was my long lost brother, Lenny. I haven't seen him in over 15 years!" stated Georgie.

Sedone turned and gave Dante a nod.

"So you never saw this ring before? Can you tell me why you haven't seen Lenny in such a long time, he "is" your brother?" questioned Sedone.

"When he was fifteen, Lenny stole my life savings from me, and tried to pin it on my little brother.

When I figured out that Lenny was the thief, I gave him a pretty severe beating. He crashed through a second floor bedroom window to get away from me, and disappeared into the night and ran away. But before he left the farm, he took an axe and cracked my horse's front leg in two, as some sort of sick payback! Then he stole my dad's farm truck and took off! He got picked up the next day robbing a gas station, and they sent him straight to reform school for a couple years, somewhere in upstate New York. That was the last time anyone saw Lenny," exclaimed Georgie.

"Sounds like something sick Lenny would do," interjected Billy.

"So knowing how your brother, Lenny is, would you say he is still angry about that beating you gave him?" asked Sedone.

"Lenny was always crazy! My dad rode him pretty hard because he was such a screw up, and I think he resented me because I was the eldest son, and he definitely hated our little brother, because he felt that he was the cause of him not getting what attention was due to him.

Yeah, I would bet he is still pissed about that beating I gave him," proclaimed Georgie.

"Okay Georgie, just so you know what kind of guy your brother is.

Lenny was supposed to go back to see you at your shop tonight, and collect the money you owe me since they got nothing from you when they visited you in your store this morning. He said that you promised him money if he returned later that day, but instead he came back with a story that he beat you up and you gave him this ring to pay me off!" stated Sedone.

"Oh my goodness, Lenny did that for me!

He is not the same old Lenny, where is he? I would like to thank my brother for his help!" cried Georgie.

"Don't go getting all emotional Georgie, I want to tell you something about this ring. It belonged to my brother, Alberto. He was murdered many years ago, back in New York City. Some bastard killed him and took it off his dead finger.

When Lenny gave me this ring tonight, he made up a story and said that '*you gave it to him*', to pay off your debt with me.

Lenny knew that I would recognize the ring, and I would get very angry and want to kill the piece of shit who he got it from, because that guy killed my dear brother...Kapeesh? Do you understand?" stated Sedone.

Georgie sat there nervously sweating and looking totally confused.

"Your brother Lenny wanted us to believe that you killed my brother Alberto, and that you took this ring off his finger! He knew we would come after you, and put the worst kind of pain and suffering on you! And then kill you a thousand times!" exclaimed Sedone. Georgie sat there terrified and shaking like a leaf.

"So it's true, my father always said that "Lenny was the devil," and if he could do this to a brother, he is the face of evil," declared Georgie.

"Now Georgie, if you never saw this ring before, how do you suppose Lenny acquired it?" questioned Sedone.

Georgie nervously thought for a moment and then spoke out.

"Sedone, I haven't seen Lenny since we were teenagers and he ran away from home.

My family tried to forget him, and we never heard from him except when he first got arrested for robbing that gas station attendant.

The only thing we knew was that he was in a reform school somewhere in upstate New York and he got booted out when he turned eighteen," exclaimed Georgie.

Dante suddenly realized something, and his eyes opened wide with anger.

"Minga Sedone, I think Uncle Alberto's idiot step son Joey, the kid who was also killed in Alberto's office the same night, had done time at the reform school, it had to be about the same time Lenny was there! I remember Uncle Albert bragging about how he set up his idiot step son, to get him busted and out of his hair! They planted a car and told Joey that the keys were in it and to go steal it. A cop on the take was waiting nearby to shake Joey down for grand theft auto, but he bolted with the car, and wouldn't stop until he finally totaled the car in front of the police station. Alberto was pissed because it was his new car that he just bought for himself! They sent him to the kid's joint, somewhere in upstate New York.

Lenny must have known Joey from there, and Lenny had to be the one who whacked Alberto and the rest of his gang!" exclaimed Dante.

"Son a ma bitch! That piece of shit saved my life hours after he killed my beloved brother!" stated Sedone.

"Minga, I have a big problem now…Billy what do you think I should do?

On the one hand, that son a ma bitch killed my brother, but on the other hand, he saved my life for which I am in his debt. What am I to do??" pondered Sedone.

Billy was often helpful in these situations since he was the only one of Sedones gangsters that sometimes attended church, although it was usually only to steal from the collection basket.

"This is an easy one Sedone, you need to go with the 'Acey Ducey,'" remarked Billy.

"Acey Ducey what the hell is that!" shouted Sedone.

Dante was deliberately looking through Georgie's mail, which was piled up high in a cardboard box on his kitchen counter, mostly of which were past due bills.

Until he found a letter from his mother with her return address on the envelope, he shoved it into his pocket while Sedone and Billy spoke.

"Okay Sedone, here's how I think this should play out.

You got two cards on the table, an Ace and a Deuce.

Georgie here is just a deuce and we are going to kill him, right?" exclaimed Billy.

Just then, Georgie suddenly panicked and tried to get up but Dante waved his gun at him, and so he sat back down.

"Go on, talk," ordered Sedone.

"Lenny right now is the high card who saved your life, but he didn't do it out of the goodness of his heart, he was just at the right place at the right time. Who knows, maybe he was coming to put a hit on you too that night, but Bobby G's gang got there first.

Lenny also set us up to whack his own brother for something the schlub had nothing to do with.

I suggest we let Georgie live to pay back the life Lenny gave you. Then we hunt down that rat tailed Lenny, and make him pay the price for what he did to your brother, Alberto!" proclaimed Billy.

Sedone listened carefully and thought for a moment.

"Okay Georgie, did you hear that? Billy gave me an idea and I'm going to let you live. I'm even going to forget about the money you owe me, as to make this good with Christ for all the other bad things I did to you.

Maybe sometime you can give me a good deal on one of those color TV's you have downstairs," stated Sedone.

Georgie was relieved, but still didn't trust that Sedone might just shoot him in the back of the head anyways.

"Sure Sedone… Thanks for not killing me," Georgie cried.

Sedone gave him a pat on the shoulder as Dante came up from behind him and struck Georgie on the back of the head with the butt of his machine gun, knocking him unconscious.

"What the frig Dante!!" shouted Billy.

"Aye, fa get about it, It's in my nature, I had an itch!" declared Dante.

"You cracked his head because you had an itch?!" exclaimed Billy.

"Yeah, what's it to ya? Tie him up before I get itchy again and crack your head open too!" jeered Dante.

Billy hastily tied Georgie to his chair with an extension cord.

He was unconscious, but alive.

Chapter 31

The three men scrambled out the door with their trench coats flailing behind them, and they bolted down the stairs back into Sedone's Limo.

They sped off and began discussing their next move.

"Billy, head over to Lenny's apartment! Let's see if maybe he is hiding out there," ordered Sedone.

When the men arrived at Lenny's apartment building, and after surviving climbing the 8 flights of stairs, it was obvious that Lenny was gone.

They rummaged through his things, and his scant accommodations when Billy found the strong box, hidden under the kitchen sink.

"Sedone check this out, I found it under the sink!" declared Billy.

Sedone opened the metal box and saw that it contained a sealed glass jar of formaldehyde with a grotesque human finger floating around in it, the crumpled up picture of himself standing in front of his restaurant, and the small brown journal that belonged to his brother Big Al.

"Whose finger do you suppose that is, Sedone?" questioned Billy.

"I know who's finger it is, Billy. It's Frank the Indian's chopped off finger. Years ago, my brother organized a truce with Frank's gang to divide up territory in the City. Alberto set him up in a trap, and they ambushed Frank and his gang. Frank was the last man standing, but he was stubborn and wouldn't give up his ring when Alberto ordered him to take it off and to place it on his finger. He refused and so Alberto tried pulling it off himself, but it was too tight and he couldn't get it off of Frank's hand!" replied Sedone.

"Eeesh, I hope he killed him first, before chopped his finger off!" exclaimed Billy.

"What do you think, Stoonade? We are talking about my brother, Alberto. He wanted to humiliate Frank, and so he forced him to watch in agony as his men held his hand down on a table, and my brother victoriously chopped off his finger with a meat cleaver. When he went to pick it up off the floor, the finger was moving around as if it was trying to crawl away with the ring! My brother picked it up and stared at it in amazement, and then slid the bloody ring off of Frank's squirming finger, and forced Frank to watch as he put his prized ring on his own finger! In turn, Frank spit on my brother's face, and that infuriated him, and so Alberto picked up the meat cleaver again and split his head open like a melon!" stated Sedone.

Billy shivered at the thought of Frank's finger squirming and crawling across the floor, as he watched Sedone reenact Frank's squiggling finger with his own finger. Sedone then picked up the crumbled picture and admired it for a moment, and stated that the picture was taken when he first opened the restaurant, many years ago.

The only other thing left in the box was Big Al's little brown journal. Sedone hesitated to pick it up, but then slowly reached in as if that box was the Holy Ark of the Covenant and the notebook was the lost stone tablets of the Ten Commandments that were etched by God himself.

"Minga, this was Alberto's booking journal!" Sedone exclaimed.

"I think that book proves one thing, that Lenny was absolutely the one who killed your brother," stated Billy.

Sedone became enraged and he picked up the metal strong box and threw it at Lenny's television set, smashing the glass screen to pieces!

"He can go buy a new television from Georgie if he survives," angrily stated Sedone.

"Where do you think he is?" questioned Billy.

"He did say he was going to visit his momma," stated Sedone.

"Let's go back and shake down Georgie, he can tell us where to find his mother's house!" remarked Billy.

"Hold up Sedone, if we go back to Georgie's place he might tip off his mother and Lenny that we are looking for him, besides I already know where she lives," proclaimed Dante.

Dante reached into his coat pocket and pulled out a crinkled up envelope, and handed it to Sedone.

Sedone glanced down at it, only to find it was a letter from Lenny's mother, with her return address written on it.

"Dante, you don't miss a beat!" chuckled Sedone.

"You mean, I don't miss a beating!!" arrogantly stated Dante.

The three men quickly left the building, and commented that it was much easier going down the 8 flights of stairs than going up them!

"Billy, go get the car, we're going to Binghamton, New York!" shouted Sedone.

Chapter 32

Billy quickly appeared with the Limo and pulled up next to the curb with a screeching stop!

Dante and Sedone once again jumped in the back seat, and Billy waited for instructions on where to go.

"Sedone, what do you say we drive by the club and pick up my dad to join in on the fun?" suggested Dante.

"Great idea, my brother should be with us when we torture and assassinate our brother's killer...Billy, first go to the Italian club!" ordered Sedone.

"Whoa, whoa, whoa...whoa! I ain't going if Angelo is coming with us! Dante is a sadistic nutcracker killer and Angelo is a hundred times worse! Together, that father and son combination is way too violent and insane for this Black man to survive a ride all the way to Binghamton, New York! Besides, I don't like it when they look at me and then say stuff in Italian and then laugh! I ain't going if Angelo is coming with us, no friggin' way!" cried Billy.

Sedone paused for a moment;

"Okay, shut up and get out of the car! Then go find a payphone and call the boys. Have them pick you up with the box truck, and then go to Georgie's TV store and clean out everything that will fit into the truck. Pick out a couple of those new color televisions, the ones with the clicker so I don't have to get up to change the channel and drop them off at my house.

The rest of the stuff, hide in the warehouse," ordered Sedone.

Billy happily scampered out of the car, and Dante took over in the driver's seat, and they drove off to the Italian Club to pick up Angelo, his father.

When they arrived, Dante marched up the several granite steps to the entrance of the Italian club, and entered the building as Sedone waited impatiently in the car.

The room was full of a variety of Italian and Sicilian men socializing, and oddly they were all mostly dressed in the same ominous dark suits, wearing dark fedora hats and smoking cigars. The club seemed to be neutral ground for many of the various mobsters that lived in the area.

They were carrying on, playing cards, eating and drinking at their tables and some were sitting or standing at the bar.

There were no women allowed in the club except for the two stripper waitresses that were cajoling with the men for tips.

Angelo was sitting at a table playing poker with a few gangster looking thugs when Dante interrupted his hand.

"Padre, come on, we've got to go take care of something," Dante discreetly stated.

"Minga, can't you wait a minute! I need to play out my hand here!" barked his father.

"Go ahead with your son, Angelo. Before you lose all your money," jabbed one of the men.

Angelo placed his cards face down and coldly stared at the man, and he slowly stood up as if he was going to fight the man over what he had said.

Then suddenly Angelo put his hand inside his coat, and drew out a large caliber black pistol and aimed it at the man's face!

"What did you say to me, pezza di nerda?!!" shouted Angelo and then he pulled the trigger!

Dante instinctively pushed his father's arm away in an attempt to stop the killing, only because they had a job to do and it would take away precious time since they would be responsible for disposing of the victim's body.

The bullet struck the man high in the shoulder, knocking him halfway across the room!

The loud "Bang" echoed throughout the building and white smoke from the gun waffed up through the air.

In an instant, at least two dozen other guns were quickly drawn and aimed at Angelo by the other club members!

Dante grabbed his father's gun from him, and pulled him out of the club before a shoot out could ensue.

Angelo was extremely upset with Dante for interfering with his fight, and struggled to get back inside to finish the man off!

Dante informed him of the news that they had found his brother's killer, and so he seemed to settle down.

"Padre, we know Lenny is the scum who killed Uncle Alberto and we are driving to Binghamton, New York to kill him!" explained Dante.

"That sack of shit, I always knew he was no good! How did you find out it was him?" huffed Angelo as his pulse began to subside.

"It's a long story, but he slipped up when he tried to frame someone else for it. A joker who happened to be his long lost brother who owed Sedone a lot of money," replied Dante.

"Okay, but after we butcher Lenny, I'm going back to the club to finish off that son a ma bitch, and next time don't stop me when I'm killing someone!" barked Angelo.

The three men drove off into the night, confident that by their own hands, Lenny would soon be dead.

Chapter 33

Lenny had been driving nonstop through the night until he finally reached Binghamton at about 4:30 in the morning.

He noticed how the town had changed over the years, but as he drove down the empty streets he remembered the old schools, stores and restaurants that he used to frequent.

It gave him a sick feeling as it reminded him of how much he really despised this town, its people, the cops and especially his family.

When he noticed the church cemetery, he drove in and parked his car a short distance from where he thought his father might be buried.

Most likely near his grandparents' graves.

With the headlights left on and beaming indirectly into the family plot, Lenny approached his family's grave site.

The headstone was simple, and made up of a gray granite that resembled most of the other headstones in the cemetery.

Lenny knelt down and read the engraved letters that were carved into the stone.

Ronald Kuhr

March 3,1897-May 22,1969
Beloved Husband and Father who loved his Family

Lenny shook his head in disbelief as he read the stone, and then spoke to his father's spirit;

"Hi Dad... it's me, Lenny. I'm sorry, I didn't realize you had so much love for me since you always treated me like shit, and I never heard from you after you turned your back on me! But I have a present for you anyways, Dad. This is for you, for my father that loved his family so much!"

Then Lenny unzipped his pants, and began urinating all over his father's grave stone.

When he was finished he pulled up his zipper and spat on it for good measure.

"Thanks for nothing you miserable son of a bitch!" Lenny shouted and then he pushed the head stone over so that the name was no longer visible as it was planted on to the ground.

"There...now I feel better! Did I piss on your grave good or did I screw that up too, Dad?" growled Lenny.

Satisfied he had the final word to his father's spirit, he walked back to his car and left the cemetery, driving off in the direction of the farm.

When Lenny arrived at his mother's house, the sun was barely coming up over the mountain, but it was still dark enough that he could not be seen.

The morning bird's subtle chirping could be heard, and some of the farm animals were beginning to rustle and move about.

When he got out of his car, he was surprised that the old house still looked the same, but some of the distant fields were now riddled with tracks of new houses.

He glanced up at the sycamore tree near the house, and noticed that it had grown some since the last time he had seen it.

Then he vaguely noticed the remnants of the twine attached to the tiny bird skeletons, which were still tangled up high in its branches.

He jubilantly smiled, reminiscing how upset Sonny had been when he began shooting those helpless birds as they were tangled up in that tree.

He slowly approached the old farmhouse, and walked up the steps to the porch and opened the front door.

As he entered the house, its pungent smell sparked his memory of the time he lived there.

The house was dark as he quietly meandered through the rooms.

Things there were the same, yet different.

The same old furniture and old pictures on the walls, but now the rooms were littered with children's toys, books and pictures of Sonny with his new wife and kids.

"What a piece of shit that Sonny is...taking advantage of our poor old mother to get himself rich, and cutting me right out of my inheritance!" scowled Lenny, as he continued wandering throughout the house.

He approached the base of the staircase leading up to the bedrooms on the second floor, and placed his hand on the thick slippery railing that he had often slid down as a young boy.

He paused with a smile, reminiscing that he had once pushed Sonny over that railing causing him to cut his head open, and a visit to the hospital emergency room.

Lenny continued up the stairs to his mother's bedroom.

When he arrived at her door, it was still dark in her room, but he could vaguely see her silhouette as she peacefully slept.

He leaned up against the door jam and tossed his hat on top of a picture of his father that was framed on top of the bureau.

Contently, he watched his mother sleep as he tipped his head and smiled.

"Man how things could have been so different if Sonny never showed up around here," he thought.

He quietly moved over beside his mother, and softly bent over and kissed her forehead.

He could smell the fragrance of her, and he felt the softness of her hair.

Then instantly, it was as if his flood gates had opened and all of Lenny's pent up anger was released, and he was overcome with senseless rage!

He grabbed a pillow from the bed, and with both his hands he aggressively put it over her face, and then he placed all of his weight on it and he began smothering his mother!

She struggled to remove the pillow from her face, but she didn't realize if this was a nightmarish dream or reality.

Lenny was too strong for the aged woman to fend off, but she fought like hell to save herself!

"Hey Ma, it's me Sonny... I was really the wicked son, and Lenny was the good boy! Now I'm going to get rid of you so I don't have to take care of you anymore!!" Lenny scowled.

Then with his right hand, he reached under the pillow and took hold of her throat as she blatantly thrashed about, and he squeezed his grip as hard as he could, choking the last bit of life out from his mother!

He maniacally laughed, believing she would go to her grave believing it was Sonny that had killed her.

When she finally stopped moving, he let go of her throat and sniffed his hand as he strolled out the door of her bedroom.

He then wandered into the bedroom which he had shared with Sonny, and picked up his old wooden baseball bat which was leaning in the corner of the room.

It was worn and aged but he could still make out his name which he carved into it.

He took a few practice swings and pretended to hit a home run.

It was odd because no one could remember him ever using that bat for anything other than for beating animals senseless, considering the fact he never played a game of baseball in his life.

He pulled the sheets off his bed and pinched the corner of his old mattress and dragged it off the bed frame, and he instantly rediscovered the hole he made in it, and the secret hiding place where years ago he had stashed the money he had stolen from Georgie's safe.

He reached inside the hole and was pleasantly surprised to find that the money was still in there, and so he took it out and fanned it in the air to remove some of the musty smell, and then smirked as he stuffed it into his shirt pocket.

He then began prowling around Sonny's bed. He pretended to sneak up on his little brother, and with all his might, smash him over the head with the bat, as he soundly slept!

"Man if I could have gotten away with that, I would have bashed his brains in a thousand times!" thought Lenny.

He tossed the bat on Sonny's bed as he careened out of the room to the stairs, and awkwardly slid down the railing for old times' sake.

He clumsily dismounted the railing and then headed into the kitchen for something to eat. When he opened the refrigerator, he noticed a half eaten broiled chicken, and he tore off one of its drumsticks and placed it into his mouth as he rummaged his way out of the house.

By now the morning sun had risen and his smashed up car with out of state plates was apparent.

He thought he had better hide it, as not to give away to Sonny that someone was there. He opened the large barn doors and drove his car way into the back of the long enormous barn, and then quickly closed the large wooden doors and hid as he waited for his little brother, Sonny to appear so he could finally kill him.

Chapter 34

The three mobsters finally arrived in Binghamton the following morning when Sedone woke up.

"Minga Sedone, you snore like a friggin' elephant!" exclaimed Dante.

"Never mind, wise guy, how much farther is it to the farm?" yawned Sedone.

"This map says we should be there pretty soon," said Dante.

"Okay, so let's make a plan. How are we going to get Lenny?" questioned Sedone.

"That's easy, I think I'm going to jump him and tear his head off! I always wanted to rip someone's head right off their neck!!" exclaimed Dante.

"Dante, fugget about it. It sounds like fun but I tried that once when I lived in Sicily. There's too many strings in the neck that hold on the head, you're gonna need a knife or a saw," remarked Angelo.

"Dad not for nothin', I think I'd like to give it a try. I think if I twist it around a few times I can get it off!" joked Dante.

"Yeah, good luck wise guy," whispered Angelo.

"Listen you two, I think I should just whack him over the head with a pipe the way he killed Alberto, then Dante you can try to pull off his head if you want!" chuckled Sedone.

"Yo, here comes the street we're looking for," stated Dante as he folded up the crumbled map.

"Drive by the house and see if Lenny's car is there," ordered Sedone.

They slowly drove past the farmhouse, back and forth several times, but there was no sign of Lenny or his car.

Lenny was perched up in the hayloft of the barn, peering out through a small hole in the wall when he suddenly recognized Sedone's Limo pass by.

"Ho-ly-shit!! I figured that they would have just ambushed Georgie and killed him, no questions asked. They must have held off and questioned Georgie about the ring, and put it all together that it was me that whacked Big Al, and they drove all the way over here to kill me!" Lenny thought.

Lenny quickly scurried down from the hay loft on a frail wooden ladder, and he snatched up the Tommy gun from his car and snapped on a drum of ammunition.

"Dante let's go see if Lenny's mother knows where he is, pull into the driveway and park behind that old shed," ordered Sedone.

Dante drove into the gravel driveway, and parked behind the storage shed while Lenny observed them through one of the many holes and crevasses in the old barn's wood walls.

The three men looked out of place on the farm in their gangster attire as they got out of their car, stretched and surveyed the area for any signs of Lenny.

They covertly shuffled over to the house, and stopped at the base of the porch steps, and then cautiously continued up and approached the front door.

Dante then pulled open the screen door and lightly tapped on the old wooden farm door with his gun.

After a few moments when no one answered, Dante prepared to kick the door in.

"Hold up Dante. Try turning the knob first," said Sedone.

Dante made a look of doubt, but then turned the knob and surprisingly the door opened.

"We are out in the country here, nobody locks their doors," remarked Sedone.

Angelo and Dante cautiously entered the house, searching for Lenny with their guns drawn, while Sedone made himself comfortable, and sat down on an old rocking chair and waited on the porch.

"Dante, this house stinks like cow shit!" complained Angelo.

"Minga, who the hell would want to live out in the sticks like this? Fugget about it!" exclaimed Dante as they wandered through the house.

They inspected each room in the house searching for Lenny, and after a few minutes they returned to Sedone, who was slowly rocking in the rocking chair on the porch.

"Lenny's not here, Sedone. But his mamma is upstairs, dead in her bed with a pillow over her face. But look what we found up in the old ladies bedroom…Lenny's hat!" exclaimed Dante.

"Son o ma bitch! That scum killed his own mother…on her birthday no less!" exclaimed Sedone.

"Okay, this guy needs to be killed. Let's go find this piece of garbage and show him how we take care of things the Sicilian way!" exclaimed Angelo.

Angelo turned around and marched back inside to the kitchen. He took an oversized butcher knife and its steel sharpening rod and returned to the porch.

Then he began rhythmically crisscrossing the blade over the steel rod, honing the knife to a razor's edge.

"Any swine that kills his own mamma is going to get carved up like a pig!" scolded Angelo.

"Okay, so we know he's around here someplace, let's go find him!" ordered Sedone.

"I don't know Sedone, I have a bad feeling about this. Lenny probably already knows we're here, and he is maybe sitting up in a tree waiting to pick us off. We need to get out of the open," suggested Dante.

Just then Dante noticed tire tracks imprinted in the gravel driveway, and it led into the closed up barn.

"Minga, look at the tire tracks, Lenny is in the barn!" whispered Dante.

"Angelo, you cover the front barn door, where he went in with the car. Dante and I will flush him out from the back!" exclaimed Sedone.

The two men raced around to the back of the long barn, while Angelo stoically stood in the barnyard. Waiting in front of the barns large wooden doors, with his butcher knife in one hand, and his large semi automatic hand gun in the other, preparing for Lenny's murder.

Lenny was totally aware of what was happening, and devised a plan of his own.

Unfortunately for them, they were on his turf now, and out of their element.

Parked inside the barn, near the barn's front doors was the old John Deere tractor that Lenny used to operate, with the hay-baling machine attached to it.

When he saw that Dante and Sedone were heading to the back end of the long barn, he started the tractor and engaged the baling machine.

Angelo heard the tractor engine start, and was swinging his knife wildly in one hand and holding his cocked pistol in the other, waiting for Lenny to come running out.

"Come on out, pezzo di nerda!" Angelo shouted.

Lenny raced the engine of the tractor, revving up its RPM's and popped the clutch on the old tractor!

Its front wheels jumped off the ground, and it lurched forward as it quickly accelerated!

The tractor exploded through the old wooden barn doors, and the impact thrusted Angelo backwards down to the ground.

Lenny quickly turned the tractor and maneuvered the hay bailer towards Angelo.

Its spinning metal claws instantly snared and grabbed hold of Angelo's body, and by design, began drawing him into the baling machine.

Angelo desperately struggled to free himself, but it was impossible as the baler was unyielding and powerful!

It clung on to him and dragged him up and into its massive iron mouth, and the machine began quickly consuming him!

His agonizing screams were drowned out by the tractor's racing engine as the baler rhythmically operated and plowed him into the internal baling mechanism, cutting him into pieces, then compressing him and binding his mangled dismembered body into a bloody mess of a bale.

"Hmmm, I always wondered what this thing would do to somebody if they got sucked up into it. That was a little too disturbing, even for me. There should really be warning labels on farm equipment, these machines are dangerous!" chuckled Lenny as he jumped off the tractor and scurried back into the barn.

He grabbed a gallon of red tractor paint from a workbench and his machine gun, and climbed back up the ladder into the hay loft and hid.

When they heard the commotion, Dante and Sedone raced back to where they had left Angelo, only to find a bloody mess of Angelo's gruesome body parts all chopped up into pieces and packaged into a hideous bale and tossed on the ground from the exit port of the haybaler!

Dante was stunned and he broke down and began to sob hysterically!

"He killed my padre! He killed my padre!" Dante agonizingly screamed.

He tried to somehow take hold of his fathers remains, which were now gruesomely packaged and bundled up in a bloody bale of his father's body.

"Dante! We have to keep our heads on, there is nothing we can do about Angelo right now, let's kill that son o ma bitch, Lenny!" commanded Sedone.

Dante was distraught but managed to get back up on his feet, and he staggered towards the broken down barn doors, while Sedone headed over to the rear end of the barn in case Lenny tried to escape.

Dante's distress turned into madness, and he became enraged and began screaming at Lenny who was hiding up in the hayloft, and observing from behind a large 500 lb bale of hay.

"Hey Dante, you can use your padre's body parts and make a scarecrow that looks just like him!" snickered Lenny.

Dante fired off some shots in the direction of Lenny's voice, but widely missed him.

"Hey Dante, I just want to let you know that I always thought you were a giant Oogatz! It was really disrespectful of you yesterday when I reached out to shake hands with you in Sedone's office and you ignored my hand," shouted Lenny.

"That's because I didn't want to get shit all over my hands," shouted Dante.

Dante struggled intently to hone in on Lenny's voice coming from up in the hayloft.

He looked all around, and then took cover under the overhang that supported the hayloft, and he began firing several shots up through the floor of the loft.

Lenny could have easily taken Dante out with his machine gun, but he was enjoying this game of cat and mouse.

Bewildered with rage, Dante noticed he was standing next to an old wooden ladder that rose up through a trapdoor in the hayloft deck.

Dangling alongside the ladder was a thick, twisted hemp rope that was attached to some sort of a pulley system, which seemed to operate the trap door.

"Sedone!! I have him trapped up in the hay loft!" shouted Dante.

"Be careful Dante! It could be a trick!" faintly shouted Sedone from outside of the barn.

"Hey Lenny, why don't you just come down here and we can settle this like real men, after all you are supposed to be a tough guy!" shouted Dante.

Dante suddenly took notice of the rope dangling down alongside the ladder, and immediately took hold of it, wrapping it around his hand.

"Hey Oogatz, if I were you I would let go of that rope!" Lenny sarcastically warned.

Dante was now convinced that the rope was the way to close the trapdoor, which would eliminate Lenny's escape route.

He pulled down on the rope believing it would shut the trap door and prevent Lenny from getting away.

But something seemed to be stuck, and the rope wouldn't budge. He then wrapped both hands around the rope and jumped up and pulled downward with all his might!

Something suddenly snapped and let go from above, and instead of closing the trap door it released the locking device which held up a hay elevator platform. There were 3 massive 500 pound hay bales situated on it, and the entire platform instantly plummeted and came crashing down on top of Dante, pulverizing his body and decimating him instantly!

Sedone came charging in and began shooting up the barn with his machine gun!

He was horrified when he noticed his nephew's cockeyed motionless legs, protruding out from underneath the platform of gigantic hay bales.

"Son a ma bitch!!! I'm going to kill you!!" screamed Sedone as he relentlessly fired his machine gun up into the hayloft.

Lenny dumped over the gallon of red paint which he had carried up there with him, which then trickled down through the gaps in the hay loft floor, and then he dramatically uttered a phoney "shriek of despair."

He left his clumsy machine gun behind as he began his exit and crawled down a narrow feed chute, which led to the outside of the barn.

Lenny quickly scurried away and waited patiently as he squatted on top of an old tree stump, adjacent to the barn's shattered front door.

He calmly reached into his shirt pocket and removed a cigarette, and clumsily lit it and then he reached behind his back and took hold of Big Al's massive ornate pistol.

The shooting finally stopped only after Sedone noticed the large amount of red "blood" dripping from the hayloft above, and he believed he had finally shot and killed Lenny.

Distraught over the loss of his nephew and brother, Sedone staggered out of the barn and threw down his machine gun, and collapsed onto the cool gravel of the barnyard.

He was physically, mentally and emotionally drained, but satisfied that he was able to get revenge for the deaths of his family members, and lived to tell about it.

"Is this a bad time to order a pizza, Sedone?" snickered Lenny.

He rose up and perched himself on top of the tree stump, aiming Big Al's fancy chrome and ivory gripped pistol directly at Sedone's head, as his cigarette hung loosely in his mouth!

Sedone was vanquished and could not believe his eyes, that Lenny was still alive, and he had outsmarted him!

"I guess I got the drop on you old man," chuckled Lenny as Sedone rolled over on the gravel, and unsteadily rose to his feet, a defeated and broken man, he shook his head in disbelief.

"Okay Lenny, I give up. You win," strained Sedone with an exhausted heavy heart.

"Did you really think you were gonna come on my turf and get the drop on me, old man? That was pretty stupid, but I had a lot of fun playing with you guys. Too bad about Angelo and Dante though, but rest assured you will all have a decent burial in the shit pile behind the barn!" Lenny chuckled.

"You're right Lenny, I should have known better than to take your devious mind and murderous ability for granted," replied Sedone.

"By the way, do you recognize this big fancy gun that I'm aiming at your head, Sedone?" questioned Lenny.

"No, why should I?" sighed Sedone.

"It was your brothers. It was Big Al's gun, and I lifted it from his safe! That safe wasn't so easy to open, you know. If it wasn't for that stupid picture of his precious Castle on his wall, I never would have figured out the combination," Lenny exuberantly bragged.

"Lenny, can you please tell me how was it that this all came about, and why did you kill my brother, Alberto? I would like to know before you kill me, if you don't mind telling me?" questioned Sedone.

"It was simple, I was locked up in an upstate New York reformatory where I met Joey, Big Al's stepson. Joey invited me to New York City when I got out of the clink, and he told me that Big Al might offer me a job to work in his gang. He picked me up at the train station that night, and we drove right over to his restaurant, in Little Italy. Big Al was there stuffing his fat face in the back room with two of his guys. Right off the bat, he was rude and disrespectful to me, on account of I was friends with Joey, and he hated Joey. They started making fun of me, calling me names and laughing their asses off! I couldn't take it anymore, so I left for the can. That's when I saw the pipe hanging from the ceiling. I kept hearing their hurtful words in my mind, and it reminded me of what my father used to say to me when I was a kid, and I lost my temper. When I went back to their table, 'Ka-pow!!'. All you can eat spaghetti and meatballs all over the walls! All I wanted was a dirty and dishonest job from him, but instead he ridiculed and made fun of me, along with his two other fatso's!" gripped Lenny.

Sedone just stood there listening, as he contemplated any option to save himself.

"Lenny, I'm sorry to hear that my brother treated you that way, and now I understand the reasoning for his death. But I treated you well all these years. Like my own son some of the time. I am an old man, and I believe you are going to kill me. But before you do, I am begging you, can you give an old man a last request?" questioned Sedone.

"You treated me like shit, Sedone. The only thing I got from you was 'All the shitty pizza I could eat!'. Do you want to know somethin', Sedone? Your pizza sucks and I hated it! But you're right, I am going to kill you, and you can rest in peace that when I go back to Chicago, I'm gonna take over the whole operation in your place, and then I'll finally be the boss! I suppose for all that free disgusting pizza, the least I could do is to listen to what your last request is, as a going away to hell present," Lenny sarcastically stated.

"Thank you Lenny, all that I ask is that I would like to die with my rosary beads in my hands, and pray to God that he will forgive my sins and not send me straight to hell, like you just said. They are in my car, in the glove compartment," begged Sedone.

Lenny thought for a moment, and was intrigued by Sedones' request.

"Sure Sedone, but first toss me Big Al's diamond ring so I don't have to chop it off your shriveled up finger, like your brother had done to Frank the Indian," chuckled Lenny.

Sedone twisted the ring off his finger and tossed it to him, and Lenny smirked as he triumphantly placed it on his own finger.

"It looks better on me, don't ya think Sedone?" boasted Lenny as he admired it in the sunlight.

Sedone just stood there, looking defeated and was a beaten man.

Lenny had expected that there was a gun in the glove box, but it would have been just too easy shooting Sedone in the head as he stood there hopelessly in the barnyard.

Lenny was always up to playing some sort of hideous assassination game to amuse himself, especially if it involved pain and suffering for his victims, and that morbid energy was extremely gratifying for him.

"Sure, go ahead Sedone, but no funny business though," comically stated Lenny.

Sedone staggered towards his car as Lenny followed closely, keeping his gun pressed into Sedone's back.

When they reached his limo, Sedone paused then slowly opened the passenger door. To his dismay, he noticed the keys were not in the ignition and most likely squashed along with Dante, annihilating his quickly thought out plan of an attempt to knock down Lenny, and using the Limo as a quick getaway car.

"Minga, did Dante really believe someone was going to steal the car out of this hicks driveway!" Sedone tragically thought.

"Easy does it, Sedone," warned Lenny as he noticed Sedone contemplating.

Sedone took a heavy breath, then cautiously turned sideways and sat down on the edge of the passenger seat, and slowly opened the glove box, as Lenny firmly held the gun against the side of Sedones head.

Inside the glove box was a small chrome semi automatic pistol, and a large strand of black and white rosary beads, from which hung a colossal silver tubular crucifix.

"Hold it, Sedone!" ordered Lenny.

Lenny pressed his gun harder into the side of Sedone's temple, and then reached in and took the small gun from the glove box, and tucked it behind his back.

"Okay, now you can get your beads," commanded Lenny.

Sedone slowly reached in and picked them up.

"See Lenny, this is all I wanted. Thank you, now I'm ready to die," Sedone mournfully stated.

Lenny then ordered Sedone to stand up and move away from the car.

He moved in front of Sedone at arm's length, raised the large gun and pulled back the hammer of the gleaming chrome pistol, as he aimed it right between Sedone's eyes.

"I hope this means something very special to you Sedone, that I'm going to blow your brains out with Big Al's gun," chuckled Lenny.

"Yes Lenny, thank you very much, and when I see Alberto in heaven, I'll mention to him what a nice thing you did for me, much appreciated," replied Sedone.

"I think you are being a little too optimistic, Sedone. That you and Big Al end up in heaven!" chuckled Lenny.

Sedone shrugged his shoulders, and then firmly grabbed hold of the large tubular crucifix on his rosary beads and held it so Jesus was looking right at Lenny's face.

"May I ask you for one final request, that you not shoot me in the face, and then may I say a prayer before you kill me, Lenny?" solemnly questioned Sedone.

"Sure Sedone, considering I was like a son to you, I can shoot you wherever you would like. And by the way, could you mention something nice about me in that prayer of yours too?" Lenny chuckled as he lowered his gun.

Sedone cracked a strained smile and began to pray.

"I pray to God to forgive me for all the people I killed, but please don't hold that against me, most of them had it coming, Lord. Please forgive me for the money I stole, and all the bullying I did. I apologize for cheating on my wife with her cousin, Eva. And all the other girlfriends I had on the side. I apologize for using bad words and all my selfish deeds, I'm sorry for..." Sedone rambled on.

"Alright already, Sedone, that's enough!" Lenny interjected.

"And most of all Lord...for killing this piece of shit!" Sedone shouted in anger.

At that moment, Sedone quickly flipped up the cross, exposing the open cylinder of a gun barrel at the base of the cross!

Lenny immediately realized that he had been outsmarted and the large cross was actually a single shot small caliber gun, and it was aimed right at his face!

Sedone snapped the trigger which was obscured as Jesus's arm nailed to the cross and it immediately fired a bullet that exploded into Lenny's forehead!

Lenny's finger instantly contracted from the impact, and he pulled the trigger of his pistol as he fell backwards, and he shot Sedone in the side of his torso.

In the tumult, Sedone managed to run away and he disappeared into the high grass of the meadow.

Lenny was bleeding profusely from the bullet hole in his forehead, and he became nauseous and panicked, fearing that he was done for!

He quickly got up from off of the ground and rushed into the farm house, and made his way into the bathroom to tend to his wound.

Ironically, his head pounded as if he had been cracked in the forehead with a baseball bat, just as he had done to so many innocent animals and people over the years, including old Sarg.

As he stood in front of the bathroom mirror, his face was covered with hot dripping blood! He could barely feel the bottom of the small caliber bullet round which was embedded and protruding from his forehead, and he was somewhat relieved that the bullet was obviously not powerful enough to penetrate into his skull.

He recklessly tossed the contents from the bathroom vanity drawer into the bathroom sink, and discovered an old pair of rusty toenail cutting pliers.

He grabbed at the bullet round with the slightly open jaws of the pliers, and was just able to grab hold of the base of the bullet.

With his two hands tightly clenched on the pliers, Lenny desperately began twisting and tugging at the bullet round!

The pain was excruciating, and his head waggled back and forth, and side to side as he twisted and tugged on the bullet until he finally was able to twist the mushroom shaped slug out of his forehead.

He quickly washed the blood off his face, and then broke a cigarette in half and screwed the filter end into the bullet hole to stop the bleeding.

Then he wrapped his wound by ripping a strip of cloth from a long towel, and he tightly bound it around his head.

Once again, Lenny heard his father's voice drumming into his ear as he stared at his injured face in the bathroom mirror.

"Same old idiot, Lenny! Once a screw up, always a screw up. Shot in the head by an old man with a pea shooter! You'll always be a good for nothing loser, Lenny!" drummed the voice.

Those words echoed over and over again in his head.

Lenny became so enraged that he punched his reflection and shattered the mirror, and then raced out of the house crashing right through the screen door as he left.

He desperately needed to find Sedone and finish him off before he could get away, and do it before Sonny showed up!

Chapter 35

I had left the house earlier than usual that morning. I had a meeting with some contractors about a new development we were planning in the next county over.

The plan was to be back home early enough to take my family to the lake for the day, and celebrate my mother's birthday there.

The lake was a peaceful place, and the kids enjoyed swimming and fishing there while we sat on the shore and encouraged them to "hook a big one!" Ironically, it was also a place of dreadful and horrific memories for me, mainly because I almost died there.

During the summer when I was a child, my family and I routinely visited the lake to swim and fish too, but I refused to enter the water while Lenny was in the lake swimming, unless Georgie or my parents were there with me.

I was terrified of being alone in the water with Lenny. I would have rather swam in a pool filled with great white sharks, than to be left alone with Lenny in the lake.

He constantly antagonized me there, and told me stories about the kids who had mysteriously drowned in the lake, while he just happened to be there in the water with them.

Their dead bodies disappeared down into the murky depths of the lake, and then were carried off by huge snapping turtles who devoured their bones and all.

He went on to say that their mutilated bodies were never recovered, and so no cause of death, or their whereabouts could ever be determined.

"No body, no evidence of a crime," he would gloat and he would then wickedly smile and evilly wink at me, implying that he had something to do with their demise.

I didn't really believe him, since I never heard of anyone drowning there, but I believe given the chance, he would have definitely taken the opportunity to drown me, but only if we were all alone and he thought he could get away with it.

There was that one summer afternoon at the lake, when I was 10 years old, I was playing on the shore line, and searching for baby turtles hiding among the weeds on the water's edge.

My parents shouted out to me that they were going off to the store to get some ice cream and cold drinks with Georgie, and would be right back.

When Lenny noticed they had left me alone, he immediately exited the water, stating that he had enough swimming and he was going fishing down by the dam.

He collected his fishing gear and took off into the woods, where there was a dirt path that led around the lake to the dam.

That's when I felt it was safe to go into the water, when Lenny was not there.

It was so hot that day, I couldn't wait to cool off in the crisp lake water!

I scampered back to the sandy beach and dove right into the water.

Oddly, there was no one around and the beach was surprisingly empty, considering how hot it was that day.

I began swimming out to a square floating dock which was anchored about 150 feet away from the shore, and even though the water was deep and over my head, I was confident since I was a strong swimmer.

I was almost to the dock when I suddenly felt a yank on my leg as if a shark was attacking me! I paused to see what it was, and that's when I felt someone grab onto my leg! It was Lenny!!

He had covertly circled back from the woods knowing I would go swimming once he left the water!

I panicked when I saw him hideously grinning at me as he was clamped onto my leg and treading water next to me!

I knew instantly what he was there for, to drown me!

And so with my heart pounding blood through my veins, I frantically kicked my slippery leg free from him and I tried to swim away, but Lenny was relentless and a stronger swimmer than me! He heaved himself on top of me and grabbed a hold of my hair! I instantly felt an enormous rush of adrenaline overwhelm me, and I fought like hell to get away from him, but he was bigger, stronger and determined to drown me.

He managed to get behind me and he placed both his hands on top of my head, and with all his might he pushed me down and held me under the water!

I couldn't defend myself, and I panicked and thrashed about violently, desperately trying to escape his hold on me, and get back up to the air!

I totally felt that my life was over, and I would soon be dragged off to the bottom of the lake by the snapping turtles.

I continued to fiercely thrash about, and I managed to spin around and kick Lenny off me!

It was that moment when I was able to get back up to the surface, where I could get to the air and breathe again!

No sooner than I took a breath, Lenny was back on top of me once again, pushing me down and holding me under the water!

I was fighting for my life, and I could feel hot sweat pouring out of my body and into the water as I was deathly panicking and wildly fighting to escape from his grip!

I could hear him shouting down at me;

"Just relax, don't fight it, breathe the water like a fish!"

I began to gasp and run out of air! I felt my mouth beginning to draw in water, and just as my body began to go limp and I was about to black out, I felt at peace, and my body stopped thrashing and I began to sink down into the dark abyss of the lake. I was dying.

Oddly, through what little consciousness I had left, I felt a powerful force mysteriously elevate me back toward the surface.

I wasn't sure if I died and it was an angel pulling me up to heaven, but I suddenly realized that I was at the water's surface behind the dock, and able to breathe the air again!

I clung onto the dock and coughed out the water that was trapped in my lungs, and I regained my senses. I hid behind the dock as I watched Lenny vigorously swimming away back to the shore as fast as he could!

He quickly reclaimed his fishing gear and took off back into the woods, most likely to create his alibi that he was off fishing when I went into the lake by myself and drowned.

But, strangely I searched the water all around me, but there was no one there. I don't know how I survived or who brought me up to the water's surface.

All I can think of was that it was either divine intervention, an Angel sent from God who rescued me, and lifted me up to the surface, or a giant snapping turtle.

But whatever it was that saved me, the reason must have been because it wasn't my time to die.

When my parents finally returned, Lenny had it planned that he would just come walking nonchalantly out of the woods at the same time, and he was carrying a few dead fish that he had found washed up on shore along with his fishing gear.

He shouted to my parents that he had been fishing the whole time that they were gone, and to look at the fish he had caught over on the other side of the lake, by the dam!

"Mom, Dad, is Sonny with you?" Lenny then shouted to my parents as he was professing to be concerned about my whereabouts.

My parents had a grave look of concern, instantly regretting leaving me behind with Lenny.

Georgie ran towards Lenny and grabbed him by the front of his shirt and began shaking him.

"If you did anything to him, I swear I'll kill you Lenny!" Georgie barked.

"As you can see, I've been fishing the whole time you were gone, and it's not my job to watch the brat, ya meathead," replied Lenny and he harshly pushed Georgie off of him.

I was watching as I was hiding behind a nearby maintenance shed, waiting for my parents and Georgie to return.

"I'm right here Lenny, so sorry you were worried about me!" I sarcastically stated, as I came strolling out from behind the shed.

His face was mortified and in shock to see me standing there alive, as he presumed that he had drowned me, and he was finally rid of me for good!

Later that day, when we were alone, I told my parents and Georgie about what Lenny had done, and my father got so angry he took the strap to him, and gave him a pretty good whoopin'.

Lenny realized that it was his one and only opportunity to pull off my murder, and if anything else ever happened to me beyond that, they would know it was him and he would be blamed for it, whether it was his fault or not.

I was suddenly jarred out of that dreadful reminiscent daydream, when I hit a pothole in the road, and I noticed a gas station with a payphone.

I stopped and called my mother to wish her a Happy Birthday.

I thought it was odd that she didn't answer my call, but I dismissed it as the probability that she was out feeding the chickens or in the bathroom getting ready for her wonderful day.

I then called Lass, and informed her that I would be home in a few hours, and I asked her if there was anything she might need to prepare for my mom's birthday.

She reminded me not to forget to buy some party supplies and a birthday gift from the kids.

She quickly told me that she was busy preparing food and baking a cake, and had no time for chit chat.

"Love ya baby, please hurry back home," she said and then she hung up.

As I hung up the pay phone, I thought to myself;

"Man, this is going to be my mom's best birthday ever!" and I jumped back into my pickup truck and drove off.

Chapter 36

Lass had been listening to country music blaring from the radio all morning as she was preparing food for the party.

Oddly, she thought she had heard a stumbling noise at their back porch door.

When she peeked out through the back door window, she was taken aback when she noticed an old man collapsed on the porch floor, covered in blood!

She rushed outside and tried to help him, and she frantically began shaking the man, trying to wake him from his unconsciousness.

"Who are you?!! What happened to you?!!" cried Lass.

The man barely opened his eyes and tried to talk, but he had lost so much blood he could barely speak.

"Do you...have a gun?" he strained and coughed, and then he passed out once again.

She looked up and noticed the image of another man walking toward her from the meadow.

The low morning sun was at his back, and she could only identify his blinding silhouette. She didn't recognize the man, but she was desperate for anyone's help.

"Help, help!! This man is hurt!!" she called out.

The stranger casually walked over and looked down at the old man's latent body.

Lass became frightened when she suddenly noticed the stranger's bloody homemade bandage wrapped around his forehead, and the fresh blood all over his face and clothes.

Then she instantly recognized the unmistakable resemblance to her husband and she immediately knew…Lenny was back in town!

"Is there a problem here, Missy?" Lenny sarcastically questioned.

"This man is hurt and he needs help! Can you stay with him while I go inside and call for an ambulance?!" cried Lass, and she ran back into the house.

Lenny then calmly reached over the porch railing, and he aggressively yanked out the phone wires that entered the house.

"Hi Sedone, how does that bullet I popped into your gut feel?

Thanks to you, now I have a splitting headache. Ya did pull a fast one on me though, but that wasn't a very nice thing to do after I was nice enough to let you get your rosary beads and all," whispered Lenny.

Lenny then placed his foot down on Sedone's throat, and pressed down hard with the heel of his shoe directly on his windpipe, while he began fumbling through his shirt pocket for a cigarette, which he then casually lit and deeply inhaled as he looked out across the meadow.

He pressed his heel down harder, and only removed it after Sedone had finally stopped breathing, and he was dead.

Lass returned to the rear porch in a panic and reported to the man that the phones were dead!

"Sorry lady, an ambulance ain't going to be needed, because the phones ain't the only thing dead around here, the old man just kicked the bucket," remorsefully stated Lenny.

Lass became extremely upset and began to cry!

"Who are you?!" Lass demanded.

"Who am I? Who are you? Who, who, who said the owl!" chuckled Lenny.

Lenny recognized Lass from the pictures he had seen at his mother's house to be Sonny's wife.

"You're Lenny aren't you?" nervously sniffled Lass.

"Yeah, that's me...I'm the world famous master of disaster, the best that ever was and never got caught, as my associate would say.

Where's my little shithead of a brother, Sonny boy?" inquired Lenny.

"He's not here, and I don't know when he's coming back!

I'd appreciate it if you leave now so I can tend to my children, and get the police here to take this man away," anxiously stated Lass.

"Oh what's your hurry, the old guy is dead and he ain't going anywhere, and I wouldn't want to leave without visiting with my new found family members.

I'll just wait around here for Sonny to show up, and in the meantime, me and you can catch up and get to know each other.

It's been so long since I saw my little brother, he's going to "die" when he sees me!" Lenny sarcastically chuckled.

He then pulled out Big Al's pistol and motioned for her to go back into the house.

Lenny followed closely behind her, back into his brother's home, where he found himself surrounded by more pictures of his family members which made him very uncomfortable.

"What's going on here, no pictures of Uncle Lenny?

Tisk, tisk, tisk. Now, that really hurts my feelings. Go get the kids, I want them to meet their long lost Uncle Lenny!" Lenny demanded.

"They are still asleep, please don't wake them!" begged Lass.

"Go get them or I'll shoot them in their little wet beds!" ordered Lenny and he raised his gun.

Lass ran up stairs to the children's rooms while Lenny watched her from the base of the stairs.

She held them by their wrists as she carefully walked the sleepy children down the stairs.

"Hi brats, I bet if you are anything like your pop, you little turds are still wearing diapers," Lenny jeered.

They just stared tiredly at the floor and said nothing.

When they didn't respond Lenny became agitated.

"I'm your long lost Uncle Lenny. Did your daddy ever tell you how I used to beat the poop out of him all the time? He was a real crybaby ya know, always running to mommy!" exclaimed Lenny.

The children were still half-asleep but June the little girl finally spoke up.

"Are you Lenny the loser?" she sleepily inquired and she held her nose and made a smelly face.

Lenny immediately marched over to the little girl and smacked her across the face as hard as he could with the back of his hand!

Lass tried to intervene, but Lenny punched her in the stomach and knocked her to the floor!

She had the wind knocked out of her and she was paralyzed on the floor trying to catch her breath, and then slowly she struggled to get back on to her feet.

The little girl's face had turned bright red where Lenny had struck her, but she stood her ground and she didn't waver or cry. Instead she squinted her eyes and clenched her fists.

"My Daddy's coming, and he's going to break you into a million pieces!" she shouted.

Lenny went at her again, but Lass managed to struggle over and she shielded the children from Lenny.

"We'll see about that, you little twerp! Everybody on your feet, we are going for a walk," Lenny stated.

He motioned his gun toward the door.

"Move it!" he ordered.

They headed out of the house and marched across the meadow back toward his mother's farm.

Lenny followed closely behind, constantly scanning the area for Sonny, and browbeating Lass and the children to go forward.

When they approached his mother's house, Lenny once again glanced up into the sycamore tree, and saw the twine and skeletons of the tiny sparrows.

"Hey kids, I have a game we're gonna play!" exclaimed Lenny, and he pushed them towards the slaughterhouse.

Lass tried to remain calm, but when Lenny slid open the heavy metal sliding door of the slaughterhouse, the distinct smell of death overwhelmed her.

"Please Lenny, these children are innocent! You can do whatever you want to me, but please let the children go!!" begged Lass.

"Shut up and get in there, or I'll shoot the little shits right now!" Lenny shouted.

He pushed them into the cold and wet kill room, and followed right behind them. Then he turned back and he slid the heavy metal sliding door shut.

The room was big and had an echo to it. The ceiling was very high and open and you could see the rafters above and they were loaded with brown dusty cobwebs and abandoned birds nests.

On the wall, there was a rack with rows of large iron meat hooks and an assortment of binding chains.

The floor was made of grooved concrete, and it gently sloped to a metal drain in the center of the floor, where the animal's blood would run off to.

The walls were riddled with bullet holes, and from the ceiling hung an electric winch with a long steel cable and a meat hook attached to the end of it.

The controller switch hung down from it, and the winch was positioned on a trolley so that it could be maneuvered around the room.

The slaughterhouse hadn't been used since Sonny's father had died.

It was a common event that his father would slaughter animals, after all it was a farm and that's what the animals were raised for.

Lenny grabbed two binding chains hanging from an iron meat hook, and ordered Lass to fasten each of the chains around each of her ankles, and to also fasten the opposite ends of the two chains to each of her children's ankles. Shacking Lass together with her children so that their legs were all chained and tethered together.

"Since I'm so bored, and I really don't like you or your kids, we're going to play a little game I invented called "As the sparrows fly."

Here's how it works. I'm going to open up the door and the three of you are going to make a run for it. If you 're lucky, you might just get away, otherwise... ughh, it's going to be really messy. If I were you though, I would make sure that I run really really fast, as fast as you can and whatever you do, don't trip!" chuckled Lenny.

Lass pushed the children behind her and tried to reason with Lenny.

"What kind of man would murder innocent children in cold blood? Let the children go and you can kill me," she cried.

"I'm going to kill you anyway, where is the incentive here? But before I kill Sonny, I want him to see that I took everything away from him. Especially his wife and kids!

By the way turd nuggets, your Granny is with GrandPappy now in hell, and she said she really hated you kids, and it was all your fault that she died!" jeered Lenny.

The children began crying, and Lass tried to console them, but they were helpless and terrified of Lenny.

"No more milk and kookies!" mocked Lenny.

"Lenny what kind of an animal are you! Don't you have any conscience or empathy? These are innocent little children for God's sake!" Lass pleaded.

"It's nothing personal, Sissy. Wait a minute. It is personal but if it makes you feel better, no I don't have a conscience or empathy.

In fact, I'm going to actually enjoy killing you and those two little Lenny haters. But to show you that I do have a tidbit of heart, I'm gonna shoot you first, then you won't have to watch when I snuff the kiddies," snickered Lenny.

He pushed them closer to the doorway, and put his hand on the release lever of the sliding door and paused.

"Ya know the worst thing that ever happened to me, Sissy…It was the day Sonny was born," scolded Lenny.

Lass's heart pounded as adrenaline pumped through her veins.

"Lenny, I just want to ask you one thing before you kill us.

Was it you that took Georgie's college money, and then you broke his horse's leg??" Lass desperately questioned.

Lenny turned to her, paused and then smirked;

"Yeah…of course it was me who stole the money! Who else would a done it?" he bragged, and he reached into his shirt pocket and revealed the large fold of old musty money.

"Georgie's stinkin' money was still in my mattress where I hid it!!" Lenny proclaimed as he stuffed the money back into his shirt pocket.

Then he lifted the iron door handle with his left hand, as he kept Big Al's gun trained on them with his other hand, and he began to shove the heavy sliding door across it's rusty track, until it was wide open.

Chapter 37

I had just stopped at a five and dime store to pick up the supplies for the party, when I suddenly noticed a large snow globe with a tiny farmyard inside, sitting on a shelf.

I picked it up and gave it a shake. The snow instantly began stirring up inside the globe, and it created a snowy winter farm scene.

"My mom would love this thing," I thought, and it would make a wonderful birthday gift for her from the kids.

I gathered up the party goods, and asked the clerk to gift-wrap the snow globe.

I was very excited about my mother's party, and I wanted to stop by her house before I went home to wish her a Happy Birthday, and spend some time alone with her before the party.

When I finally arrived at her house, I pulled into the driveway but I was perplexed to see a black limousine parked behind the storage shed and the barn doors obliterated and smashed to pieces! The tractor and hay baler were out in front of the barn and appeared to have crashed through the barn's huge double doors!

The only conclusion I could come up with was, the tractor's ignition switch must have shorted out and it started by itself, and then it ran itself through the barn doors!

I got out of my pickup truck, and cautiously approached the tractor and looked it over.

As I walked toward the tractor, I couldn't help noticing all the red fluid dripping from the hay baling machine.

"Hmmm, the hay baler must have blown a hydraulic hose?" I thought, and then I curiously walked through the broken wooden debris of the barn doors, and realized that something was terribly wrong. There was a smashed up chevy parked inside the barn with Illinois plates, and the barn was a mess.

Oddly, three massive hay bales were dropped down from the loft, and there were hundreds of bullet casings all over the ground, and the barn was riddled with bullet holes!

There also appeared to be red blood dripping from the hayloft, but no, it looked more like red tractor paint.

When I noticed the hay elevator was dropped, that caused me to investigate the release mechanism.

It was then, when I shockingly discovered a man's body, crushed beneath the three massive hay bales!

It shocked me and I didn't understand who this person was, or why this person was in our barn. But, it was clearly obvious there was some sort of gunfight that had ensued here!

"I had better check on my mom!" I thought, and I raced to her front door, only to find the screen door broken apart and off its hinges.

"Ma, Ma, where are you?!" I shouted as I entered the house. But there was no answer, and only silence.

When I passed by the bathroom, I noticed the towels and sink were laden with blood and items scattered from the vanity drawer, and there was a disfigured lead bullet on the back of the toilet.

"Something is terribly wrong!" I thought as I nervously raced up the stairs to my mother's bedroom.

I slowly entered her dimly lit room, and I could see the form of her body, lying motionless in her bed.

I broke down and began to cry! I was confused, but my only reasonable conclusion was that Lenny must have come back, since "everything turns to shit" when Lenny is around.

I picked up my mother's lifeless body and held her closely as I pressed my cheek against hers.

"I love you mom. I'm sorry I wasn't here to protect you from him," I whispered, and then I carefully laid her cold body back down on hcr bed.

Frantically, I raced downstairs and picked up the phone, and tried to call Lass.

However, all I could get was a busy signal from our phone.

Concerned for my family, I ran out the door and jumped back into my truck, and sped off down the road and circled back to my house across the meadow.

When I charged into my home, I found the house to be totally empty.

I called out to Lass, but there was no response from her or my children!

Panic-struck, I picked up the phone to call the police, but there was no dial tone and the phone was dead!

I rushed out to the back porch to check the phone wire box, and that's when I stumbled on the old man's dead body.

My heart sank, for I knew that Lenny had been in my home and my family was now in lethal danger.

I then began frantically searching for them and peered across the meadow towards my mother's house.

That's when I caught a glimpse of a man entering the slaughterhouse and sliding the door shut!

I was distraught and fearful of the danger my family was in!

It was obvious that Lenny had already killed our mother, and due to the circumstances, seemed to be on a mission to murder my family too.

Without any hesitation I ran as fast as I could back across the meadow, passing by old Sarge's grave and the old apple tree, and it reminded me what Lenny was capable of.

When I finally arrived at the barnyard, I discreetly poised myself outside the slaughterhouse door, standing flush with my back firmly against the wall.

I could hear Lenny shouting at my wife, and my children were crying.

Then I vaguely heard Lenny announce;

"Yeah, of course it was me who stole the money. Who else would a done it?!!" and then there was a short pause and Lenny spoke again. "Georgie's stinkin' money was still stashed in my mattress where I hid it," and then the heavy sliding door began to open!

I stood there motionless, my heart was pounding, as the heavy door slowly rolled towards me.

"Keep cool, Sonny. Don't lose your head!" I recited over and over in my mind.

Lenny slid the door wide open and gestured with his fancy gun to Lass.

"Run for it!" he demanded.

She tried to pick up and carry the two children, but the leg chains were too short!

"You know what Lenny …now I know why you hated your family so much! Because you were a lazy, selfish and sadistic piece of garbage! And instead of fostering a caring and loving relationship with them, you were toxic, and now look how you turned out! A worthless piece of shit!" shouted Lass.

Lenny became impatient and he shoved them out the door!

"Start runin' bitch, I'm gonna count to 5 before I start shootin'!" shouted Lenny.

He raised the fancy chrome gun out of the doorway and aimed, contemplating who he would shoot first. He kept out of sight, and remained inside the slaughterhouse as the big gun's chrome finish glistened in the sunlight, and he pulled back the hammer.

"Ooone, Twooo...!" Lenny began counting!

Lass quickly grabbed the children's hands and they began to run away!

They tripped and fell as Lass clumsily dragged them away by their arms!

Lenny counted louder;

"Threee, Fooour…!" and he began to feel for the trigger, aiming his first shot at June, the little girl!

He had lied to Lass when he promised he would shoot her first, and felt it would be more entertaining watching Lass grieve as she dragged her dead little girl along while trying to save her other child and get away.

"Run as fast as you can!!!" Lass screamed to the children.

Lenny began to maniacally laugh!

"Four and a haaalf!" he shouted, and he began squeezing the trigger!

In that instant, with all my might, I thrusted the heavy sliding door across its rolling track with such force that it caught Lenny's arm and pulverized it against the opposing door jamb, just as he was about to open fire on my family!

"FIVE!" I shouted.

The gun fell to the ground as Lenny's arm was completely obliterated and broken in half, and was freakishly dangling against the door by only its skin and muscle.

"Aaaaahh!!!!" screamed Lenny at the top of his lungs, as his arm was crushed and locked in the door!

I kept all my weight bearing against the edge of the door as Lenny tried hopelessly to slide the door over and free his broken arm!

Lass stopped running when she saw that I was there.

"Lenny is here and he wants to kill all of us!" she frantically stated.

"Take the kids and get out of here!" I shouted.

Lass quickly unshackled them, and they ran off into my mother's house, where Lass was able to call the police.

I was enraged with what Lenny had done to my mother, my wife and my children and I recounted the many years of pain and anguish Lenny had bestowed upon me.

Lenny continued screaming and swearing and was in excruciating pain as his arm was pinned by the door. He had heard my voice outside and he knew I was the one who stopped him!

I knew I had to confront him and so I thrusted the door open and was instantly face to face with my demonic brother.

"I think the world has had enough of you Lenard Kuhr," I remarked, and I punched Lenny in the face with such force that Lenny fell backwards and rolled across the concrete floor of the slaughter house.

With one powerful strike I had unleashed the pain and anger I had kept inside for all those years.

Lenny's face was obliterated from the force of my devastating blow.

He laid there on the wet concrete floor in a fetal position with his blood trickling from his pulverized face.

I walked past him and removed a chain shackle from the wall of meat hooks to restrain him until the police arrived.

Lenny was dazed, and in excruciating pain as he fumbled with his good arm to get at the small pistol that he had taken from Sedone's glove compartment, which was still tucked into his belt behind his back.

He awkwardly rolled over on the cement and drew the gun on me!

Lenny's left hand wavered as he laid on his side with his broken right arm dangling grotesquely across the cement floor!

"Hey Sonny…you grew up to be one big son of a bitch, just like Dad. But now, I'm gonna finally give you what I always wanted to, a bullet in the head! First, I'm going to blow *your* brains out! Then, I'm going outside and I'm going to kill your old lady and your rotten kids!" grunted Lenny through his agonizing pain.

I was caught off guard when I suddenly realized Lenny was pointing a gun at me, and I slowly turned to face Lenny with my hands in the air.

"Lenny, wait! I really tried to love you when we were kids, but all you ever did was shove me away and hate me. Why?" I desperately questioned.

"Because you robbed me of my childhood! When you came along, everything changed for the worst for me, and I hated you for it! Baby gets all the attention and Lenny gets the shaft! That's why I hate you Sonny!! Because of you, I was shit to mom and dad! I tried drowning you when we were kids up at the lake, and things would have been a lot better for me with you out of the picture! How many times did I contemplate holding your head under water in the bathtub or smashing your brains in while you slept. NOW, I'll FINALLY BE RID OF YOU!!" shouted Lenny.

Lenny clenched his teeth, and he angrily pulled the trigger on the gun!

I put up my hands in front of his face and cringed expecting the gun to go off and a bullet to strike me in the head!

But there was no loud bang!

In fact, there was no bang at all.

There was no bullet chambered in the gun, and with his right arm obliterated, it was impossible for Lenny to chamber a bullet!

Frantically Lenny tried to bite the breech mechanism of the gun to draw it back, but at that moment I realized the gun's chamber was empty, and I quickly fell upon him.

I put my knee on Lenny's broken arm and quickly wrestled the gun away from him.

Lenny screamed in dire agony as my knee bore down on his broken dangling limb!

"Dad was right about you Lenny…you always were a screw up. The reason you were shit to mom and dad was because...well, you are shit, not because of me!" I scolded.

Then with lack of any emotion, I stood up and attached the end of a chain shackle to one of Lenny's kicking legs, and dragged him across the kill room floor.

I reached up above my head and engaged the switch on the electric winch, and it began to lower its steel cable down to the floor, where I calmly attached the iron hook that was hanging from it to the end of the shackle chain that was securely fastened around Lenny's leg.

Lenny was screaming in agonizing pain and desperation!

Not only was he at my mercy, but this was the first time ever that I was able to stand up to him on my own. No running to my parents and no Georgie. This time it's just me and Lenny.

"I'm your Brother, I wasn't really going to shoot you, just let me go!! I Love you!!! I Love you Sonny!!" pleaded Lenny.

I knew it was all bullshit and I engaged the powerful winch and its gears began to slowly turn upward.

It slowly and effortlessly hoisted Lenny up into the air by his leg and he was hanging upside down, dangling from the winch several feet off of the floor.

As I walked toward the door, I noticed something sparkling on the floor.

It was a man's diamond ring that had slipped off Lenny's finger.

I put the ring in my pocket and walked out into the sunlight, sliding the heavy slaughter house door closed behind me.

The slaughterhouse became dead silent as Lenny hung there upside down, swinging aimlessly in a small circle.

He strained to listen to what, if anything was going on as he tried to slip out of the chain shackle which had tightened around his ankle.

Lenny assumed I had gone to check on my family and call the police and felt somewhat relieved that he was still alive.

He maniacally laughed out loud as he hung there by his leg, all alone and hopelessly swinging from the winch.

A moment later, he heard the "clinking" sound of a metal gate opening in the back of the slaughterhouse, and it echoed into the large empty room.

Then he heard the dreadful trampling and slipping of hooves on a cement floor, and loud wet snorting as if a very large animal was approaching!

Lenny was trying to swing around to see what was going on!

His eyes blurred with blood, he was mortified when he saw Big Red, the furious behemoth bull come charging into the kill room.

The smell of Lenny's blood and the innate sense of looming death that an animal perceives when entering a slaughterhouse enraged the bull as he unleashed all his aggression toward his own survival, and to kill his killer! He began to dig at the hard floor and he snorted large gobs of mucus at Lenny's dangling body!

Lenny began screaming hysterically!!

"Sonny!!!! Please help me! I love you brother!!"

The bull viciously tucked his head and charged it's 2000 lb. massive frame at Lenny's dangling body, striking him so violently, it vaulted him up into the air like a rag doll.

His body slammed up into the ceiling rafters making a loud "Thud" which echoed in the empty room and then he swiftly dropped back down like a sack of potatoes, and his body violently jerked up as the cable tightened and caught him before his head hit the floor! Georgie's stolen money ironically flew out of his shirt pocket and scattered through the air, and flew away from him like a flock of birds.

His leg was tethered by the steel cable in the same fashion as he had restrained that poor group of sparrows.

Now it was his turn to feel their pain, and what they must have endured being shackled by their binding cord, hopelessly unable to escape and tangled together way up in that sycamore tree.

The bull immediately turned his aggression back to Lenny and charged at him, pulverizing him once again up into the rafters, and then Lenny silently plummeted downward still wildly swaying and dangling there by his leg.

The bull however was relentless, and repeatedly charged and gored Lenny with his massive horns!

Lenny's screams and agonizing shrieks quickly diminished as the bull repeatedly charged back and forth with his vicious assault on Lenny, until his lifeless body finally unhooked and fell free of the winch's cable.

He dropped on his head, dead on the concrete kill floor.

Ironically he died by the horns of a bull, just like Eddie.

Chapter 38

The barn yard was now full of police cars and coroner vehicles.

I sat on the front steps of the porch at my mother's house with my two children sitting on my lap and their heads were sadly down.

Lass was beside me clutching onto my arm.

Then Ronny looked up at me and asked;

"Daddy, why are there bad people like Uncle Lenny in the world?"

I paused for a moment, and reached into my pocket.

I removed the large diamond ring that Lenny dropped on the kill floor of the slaughterhouse, and I revealed it to my two children and Lass.

"Do you see this ring kids? This is a ring that whomever is wearing it can make some people feel jealous and envious. It doesn't have to be just a ring, it could be a shiny new pickup truck and horse trailer or a big new house. It makes some people feel jealous, that they don't have what that person has, and they want that too for themselves. Uncle Lenny wore this big diamond ring to feel like a big man. It was a trophy that shouted out to everyone who saw it, that he was a bigshot and deserved respect. The bad people in the world want what others have. Money, power, material things, even love. Instead of hard work they choose to take the easy way out, and do bad things to get what they want, like stealing and hurting people. That's the only way Lenny could have acquired a ring like this. He could never buckle down and earn something on his own, when it was just easier to steal it from someone who did." I explained.

The children and Lass listened intently to what I was saying and I continued;

"That's why there are bad people in this world, kids, because bad people want to take what's not theirs, they hurt to get what they want, and do bad things to get what they believe they are entitled to. Uncle Lenny believed he was cheated out of the love and respect he thought he deserved.

He blamed others for his problems, and always took the easy way out.

His bitterness consumed his whole life. He had a thick rope tied around his leg, and he dragged around an anvil full of hate with him his whole life, but the knot was so tight that he could never untie it. Jealousy festered in him, and maybe tying those little birds together made him feel that he was not alone. Sadly, the fact was, that all he ever really needed was to hear these words from our father, which were...

"Lenny, you did good, son. I love you."

That's all he ever really wanted, but those words are now forever lost, and he never got to hear them," I stated.

I just then glanced up at the old sycamore tree, and gazed at the old twine and the tiny bird skeletons still tangled up in its high branches.

I paused for a moment, and a powerful feeling came over me.

"There is something I have to do," I stated.

I lifted the children off my lap and handed them over to Lass as I stood up.

I then marched with sheer determination toward the tool shed, and when I returned I was toting a large polished timber axe.

Everyone there including the police focused on me as I approached the old sycamore tree with my big axe.

I firmly took hold of its glossy hickory handle, and began swinging it as hard as I could, thrusting its blade into the massive trunk of the sycamore tree.

With each swing I delivered, I removed large chunks of wood from the tree trunk.

I finally felt all those years of pain and anguish leaving my body with each swing of my axe.

The tree began to crackle as it began to slowly lean into the large wedge I had hollowed out of it.

The first responders quickly noticed that the tree was coming down and they quickly began moving their vehicles out of the way!

It's branches began to sway backward as the giant tree was building up momentum for its final descent, as it began falling over towards the barnyard.

When it finally came crashing down onto the ground, the earth jogged and there was a loud thunderous thump and a violent rustling of its leafed branches crushing together.

I made my way through the fallen tree, and to the branches which embraced the entangled twine and the tiny sparrow bones which haunted me for most of my life.

I carefully removed them, and with my wife and children, we placed them in an old cigar box.

Later that day we brought the box to the shady apple tree where old Sarge was buried, and with little children's shovels, we dug a grave, and placed the cigar box into it.

I got all choked up and I became emotional and began to tear up.

"I'm so sorry little Sparrows, I didn't realize what Lenny had done to you when he asked me to set you free from the pail that fall morning, so long ago. I looked upwards toward the blue sky and I saw something there that no one else could see.

It was an Angel and she slowly raised her hands to the heavens as she was welcoming those poor little birds soles, and she lifted me up, saving me from drowning again.

But this time it was from the dark murky waters of my cataclysmic memories. Everything painful that had been built up inside of me all those years because of Lenny, was now gone for good.

I finally felt free inside. Free as the Sparrows fly…

Chapter 39

It was a blustery and turbulent rainy day back in the windy city of Chicago.

Billy Sparks had no idea of the fate of Sedone, Dante, Angelo or Lenny. However, while Sedone was out of town, why not seize the opportunity to spend a bit of quality time with Ava, Sedones mistress.

Ava had a small apartment in an old brown stone building off of Michigan Avenue.

Aside from being Sedones' mistress, she was also one of Billy's mistresses too.

They were both walking the fine line of danger.

Being caught by Sedone, would surely be the death of both of them. Nevertheless, Billy was always careful but considered the risk to be worth it, after all;

"He was the best that ever was …and never got caught!"

The torrential rain poured down in bucketfuls as Billy hoisted his trench coat over his head as he left his car, and he made his way into Ava's apartment building.

He tipped his hat low over his eyes, discreetly covering his face so as not to be recognized by anyone.

He rhythmically tap danced up the two flights of stairs and softly knocked on Ava's shoddy old wooden door.

After a few seconds the door slowly crept open, but only a tiny bit, and the security chain that was attached to it, stopped it from opening anymore.

Ava peeked out through the narrow opening at Billy.

"What the hell are you doing here?! Sedone is in my bedroom!" Ava anxiously whispered.

Billy knew she was lying, since he knew that Sedone was out of town, in Binghamton with Dante and Angelo.

"Gee Whiz…..thanks for the warning baby, I better get the hell out of here!" exclaimed Billy and he turned away and took a few steps, then quickly turned back toward the door, and hit it with his shoulder, breaking the chain clean off from the door jam!

The door suddenly burst in, and knocked Ava back and she tumbled backwards falling onto the couch!

"Party Time!!" sounded Billy as he strutted in.

"What the hell Sparks, can't you take a freaking joke!" scolded Ava as she collected herself.

"Shut up! I knew you were full of it, because Sedone is out of town…hunting," remarked Billy.

"Hunting? The only thing I ever saw Sedone hunt was skirts and money," stated Ava.

"Well you won't be seeing Lenny hanging around the school yard anymore. Remember that night when Bobby G's gang had us up against the wall, and then Lenny showed up and stole the show. He had just come from New York City and he was the dude that whacked Sedone's brother, Alberto. We figured he was coming to get a big score out of Sedone, but got sidetracked when he walked in on Bobby G's party.

Billy scooped her petite body up off the couch, and carried her into the bedroom, and closed the bedroom door with her foot.

Chapter 40

A dark and ominous figure wearing a soaking wet black trench coat, with their head covered by a large brimmed fedora hat cautiously entered Ava's apartment building.

Quietly marching up the stairs, as not to draw attention until they were finally standing outside Ava's apartment door.

The door was slightly ajar, and the broken security chain was just dangling there.

A black glove slowly rose and gently guided the broken door open.

Billy's unmistakable laughter, small talk and music from a small transistor radio could be heard coming from the bedroom as the intruder ventured in.

Billy was rambling on to Ava.

"I'm the best that ever was, Baby…best you ever had too!" bragged Billy.

The black glove carefully reached down to the doorknob of Ava's bedroom and slowly began to turn the handle, as not to draw any attention toward it.

As the bedroom door began to creak open, the light from the living room cascaded around the dark figure standing in the middle of the bedroom doorway.

Billy and Ava were startled, as they were caught by surprise in bed together!

The two were paralyzed as they both gazed up at a double barrel sawed-off shotgun, which was being aimed down at them by their intruder.

The black gloved finger jerked back on both triggers of the shotgun, firing both barrels at Billy and Ava!

Billy never even had a chance to talk his way out of this dire situation.

Their bodies were obliterated, and they fell over upon each other as they were catapulted backwards against the bed's ornate headboard.

The assassin then tossed the spent shotgun onto the bed, and then passed through the heavily wafting gun smoke, and instinctively reached down to pick up Billy's red plaid suit from the floor, carefully folding it and placing it neatly on the chair of Ava's makeup table.

As the assassin began to exit, she turned back at the blood soaked bed and their gruesome lifeless bodies, and paused for a moment.

With clenched teeth and anger in her heart, his wife uttered these words,

"Billy Sparks...The best that ever was... he just got caught!!"

And Billy Sparks finally achieved his boyhood wish… To touch the sky.

Made in the USA
Middletown, DE
23 December 2024